THE
MOONFELL WITCHES
FIRST YULE

TJ GREEN

The First Yule

Mountolive Publishing

Copyright © 2023 TJ Green

All rights reserved

ISBN eBook: 978-1-99-004768-8

ISBN Paperback: 978-1-99-004769-5

ISBN Hardback: 978-1-99-004773-2

Cover design by Fiona Jayde Media

Editing by Missed Period Editing

Contents

One

December 2023

Morgana Cornelius added another herb to the large pot simmering on the hob top and uttered the final words of the spell.

The deep purple potion began to bubble, releasing a peppery-sweet scent that she inhaled with pleasure. *Perfect*. It needed to simmer for an hour, and then she could decant it into the waiting jars. *Another job almost done.*

She wiped her hands on her apron, surveyed the large, ground floor kitchen, and winced. *Wow*. It was a mess. She'd been so caught up in preparing the potion that she hadn't cleaned as she worked. The gorgeous room with its high, Gothic windows, black-tiled walls, and state of the art appliances looked grubby. This particular potion, good for truth seeking and clarity, demanded exact timing on everything. It didn't help that the next day was Yule, she had a long list of things to do, and she was listening to jazzy Christmas songs. They had added to her distraction. Well, she had no excuses left now.

She started to clear away the jars of dried herbs, fresh cuttings, crystals, and other spell ingredients, and closed her large kitchen grimoire. She had started this book as a teenager, and it bore traces of all the spells within it. Scents filled its pages, as well as sticky fingerprints, scrawled notes in the margins, and the occasional dried crumb.

The grimoire contained spells for potions, food, teas, tinctures, and balms. The cinnamon rolls that were cooling on the tray was a recipe she had refined over the years. Food that would cheer their visitors and put them in the Yuletide mood. Not that they would need much help with that. Yule was always a big event at Moonfell, and very much looked forward to.

A flurry of activity beyond the window caught her eye. Hades, Birdie's Savannah cat, was stalking the pigeons again. He was a huge beast. Twice the size of a normal domestic cat, his beautiful, silver-spotted coat was bright against the winter garden.

She rapped the glass, and he looked up at her with his intelligent, amber eyes. Morgana shouted at him. "Hades! Behave."

The pigeon fluttered off and Hades gave her a disdainful look. Morgana accepted that cats killed wildlife, but she didn't particularly like to watch it happen. There was plenty of garden where Hades could track and kill to his heart's content. He swished his tail and vanished into the shrubs.

"Honestly, Morgana," Birdie said from behind her, making her jump, "I don't know why you bother. He'll just catch it later."

Morgana turned to her grandmother, annoyed. "There is no need to be so quiet. You nearly gave me a heart attack."

"I wasn't quiet. You have your music up at a ridiculous volume." Birdie turned the sound down with a flick of her wrist. "That's better. And you've made cakes. Lovely."

"They're for this afternoon!"

"But I should test one, just in case!" She smiled as she pinched one and took a bite. "Delicious." With her other hand, she pushed her long, grey hair back behind her ear, her messy bun not really holding much of her hair in place at all.

Morgana smiled as she took in her grandmother's appearance. "I still can't get over how you look. It's incredible! You look amazing!"

Birdie considered her reflection in the window. "I know. I can hardly believe it myself."

It had been only days since the Goddess had gifted Birdie twenty years or so of her life back. A gift given while they were exorcising a splinter of the Fallen Angel, Belial, from a woman called Olivia. An exorcism that had been very difficult. More so than they had let on to Olivia, Harlan, and Maggie, who had been involved at the time.

Maggie Milne was the Detective Inspector of the Paranormal Policing Division, and Olivia Jameson and Harlan Beckett were collectors for The Orphic Guild, an organisation that found occult items for their wealthy clients. Over the course of one such acquisition, Olivia had found jewels belonging to a Fallen Angel. Like anything attributed to the Fallen, it was powerful, beautiful, and quite toxic. Olivia had been lucky that Odette, Morgana's cousin, had spotted the splinter so soon.

The exorcism's one unforeseen consequence was that the Goddess had been unexpectedly generous. All of the witches had been granted a more youthful appearance. For Odette, the youngest at thirty-one, the effects were less noticeable, but Morgana was forty-three and had noticed a tightening of her own jawline, a smoothness to her skin, and a fresh bloom across her cheeks. There was even a bounce to her long, dark hair—although, she was grateful that she still had the grey streak. She liked it. It reminded her of the spell that went wrong.

However, for Birdie, the change had been startling. She was no longer a bent and wizened 88-year old, with cataracts and arthritis. She appeared to be a vibrant sixty-something, with great hair, skin, and teeth—and her sight fully restored. She still had silvery-grey hair, but it was thick and luscious, making Birdie look regal, especially wearing a dark red dress as she was now.

"There will be a cost," Birdie added, referring to her appearance. "And it will come soon."

"Not necessarily. The Goddess is no fan of the Fallen. And Olivia is pregnant with a Nephilim's child. She wanted to save her and the child. This was our reward." But even as Morgana said it, she felt uneasy.

"You are not that naïve," Birdie said, crossly. "There is always a price."

"It's Yule tomorrow. We'll give thanks like we always do. Well, more than normal, obviously, as we're celebrating the anniversary of owning Moonfell!" Just the thought of it made Morgana re-evaluate her list. She had a mountain of baking and cooking to do. More of their family were turning up, either later that day or tomorrow morning. The normally calm atmosphere of Moonfell would be completely turned on its head.

Birdie brushed the crumbs from her fingers and leaned against the counter to look at Morgana. Her grandmother was a force of nature, even when only days ago every bone in her body creaked and she could barely see. Her magical energy was huge. Now that she was back to her formidable self, Morgana could feel the power rolling off her. "Five hundred years of owning Moonfell. I wonder if Sibilla ever thought it would be in the family for that long? I mean, I know she bound the house to the family, but anything could have happened! A whole generation might have died in a freak accident!"

"Or a fight with demons."

"Or witch hunters," Birdie added, her expression brooding.

"But we're still here, despite all of those possibilities." Morgana finished stacking the washed dishes and started to hunt out the ingredients for the beef stew for that night's meal.

"Not just possibilities! Actual events. It's a good job we are such powerful witches."

"I sometimes think that brings its own issues."

"You cannot have light without the dark," Birdie pointed out. "By the way, did I mention that your father is arriving tomorrow?"

Morgana groaned. "You kept that quiet!"

"No, I only found out this morning. He said he'd rearranged his schedule so he could attend our celebrations after all. He said it was too important to miss."

"Sure, he did." Her father, Armstrong, was not averse to drama. "Did you tell him about all *that*?" Morgana gestured at her, taking in her face to her feet.

"No. I thought it would be a nice surprise."

"You just love to see people's reactions!"

"Wouldn't you?"

"I guess so. There'll be a lot of them. I hope you're prepared."

Her great-aunt Hortense, Birdie's sister, who was commonly called Horty, and Odette's father, Uncle Ellington, were also attending. Horty would arrive with her grandson, who was called Giacomo, later that afternoon.

"I also have news," Morgana informed her as she grabbed some onions from the fridge. "Lamorak is coming." Lamorak was Morgana's son, named after one of King Arthur's knights. As she had been named after the witch in the King Arthur tales—her father was a huge fan, and had called her younger brother Merlin—it seemed only right that she kept the tradition in the family. It had been a big name for a baby. The original Lamorak was Pellinor's son, and was one of Arthur's strongest and most fierce knights. At the age of twenty-one, he had finally grown into his name.

"Lam's coming? Now who's keeping secrets!"

Morgana walked over to the copper pot on the hob and stirred the potion widdershins. The colour was changing to a rich pink now. *Perfect, so far.* "I only found out this morning, too. He phoned to say he wanted to celebrate Yule with us. I admit, it was unexpected. His father is going away, and he didn't want to go with him." Morgana kept her eyes on the pot, hoping the next few days would be everything she hoped, and unable to meet Birdie's eyes.

Birdie swept behind her, arms wrapping to encompass her in a swift hug. "It will be fine. Lamorak is his own man now, able to make his own decisions, and not listen to his father's bleating. He'll be finishing university next year, and then, well, who knows what he might do." Birdie turned Morgana to face her, and her eyes were bright. "Everything will be fine. He asked to come here. He could have gone anywhere else. Isn't that right?"

"Yes, true. But..."

"No buts. You and his father may be at odds, but that's old news. It will be a chance to see how his magic has developed."

"If he wants to talk about it. He often doesn't."

"People change. And we're celebrating a special occasion! This could be the perfect time to discuss it."

Morgana only had one child. She had never wanted more—odd, perhaps, for a woman who helped others with their fertility issues, but one child was enough for her, and she was happy with her decision. But when she split from Lewis, his father, Lamorak had been only eight years old, and he had opted to spend more time with him than at Moonfell. She couldn't blame him. The place was overwhelming. Moonfell was something you either embraced wholeheartedly or ran away from. It was too much for some family members—even children, who had lived there for years. For her it was the only home she had known, apart from a few years spent at university a long time ago. Lamorak's father was not a witch, and Moonfell and magic had been too much for him eventually.

Morgana focussed on the present. "Perhaps he does wish to embrace his magic. We shall see."

"That's my girl. Now, where is Odette?"

"I believe she's at the New Moon Gate."

"Then I'll leave you to your potion and go see her. And then I suppose I should make sure all of the rooms are ready for our guests," she said, heading to the door on the far side of the kitchen that led to the glass house.

"Have you finished dressing the Christmas trees?" Morgana called after her.

But Birdie had already vanished, leaving Morgana to her thoughts.

One of Odette's responsibilities at Moonfell was care of the four moon gates that were situated around their sprawling garden. It was a job she adored.

The moon gates roughly aligned to the four main points of the compass, but were named after the phases of the moon. They all offered tantalising vistas into other areas of the garden.

The gates were constructed out of different materials—some of stone, some of plants—but the Waning Moon Gate that lay to the west was made of bronze. It was an enormous construction, with thick pieces of metal wrapped and bound together to make interesting shapes—owls, faces, animals, flowers. The whole thing had a rich patina bestowed by time, and was covered in jasmine that cast its scent far and wide in the summer. It was this that she was trimming, as well as cutting back the thick planting around it. Those were night-blooming flowers that would glow in moonlight.

The view through the New Moon Gate was either of the west side of the house through a glimpse in the thick shrubbery, its towers reaching into the sky, or the pond that was situated between the gate and the far perimeter, the summer house on its far bank. In the summer, the pond was thick with birdlife, insects, and plants, but it lay like a dark glass now, reflecting heavy, thick clouds that promised more snow. A flurry had already fallen overnight.

But the gates didn't just offer framed views of the garden. They provided glimpses to other things, too—if you knew how to look, and she did. Odette could see to the truth of things. Sometimes it was a dark gift. Intrusive. She couldn't help it. It had been granted to her by the Goddess, a gift at birth, and nothing Odette could ever do would make it go away. But at other times, the gift was fun—like seeing Nahum the Nephilim's wings as clear as day when he visited Olivia at their house. That was funny. It wasn't so funny, though, to see Belial so clearly when they banished him.

Her gift meant that sometimes the moon gates offered her flashes of things: the future, the past, spirits, different seasons—as if time shifted within them. They weren't portals, though. She couldn't step through them into another place or time, which was obviously a good thing. Nothing good ever came of meddling with the past.

Odette clipped off the last of the wayward strands of jasmine, dropped her secateurs on the ground, and pulled her gloves off. She stepped back to assess her work, noting the symmetry of the plants and the ancient moss that climbed over part of the gate.

And then she blinked as the air shimmered, and the view seen through the gate shifted. A woman stood on the other side, with soft blonde hair and a simple, long gown—Medieval, Odette was sure. She was hurrying towards the moon gate, her face creased in concentration, something clutched in her hands.

Odette's breath caught in her chest. The woman was indistinct—a shadow cast on the present, as was the garden behind her, but it bore only a faint resemblance to the garden it was now. A thick grove of trees was behind her. This was a glimpse of the house from a long time ago.

Then, as quickly as it had appeared, the shimmering vanished, and the pond and the summer house returned. A few seconds later, Birdie moved into view on her right.

"You saw something," Birdie said softly, as if scared of breaking the mood.

Odette stared through the gate for a while longer and then faced her grandmother. "A woman wearing an old, Medieval-style dress. The garden was different. Lots of trees." She filtered through images of past witches she was familiar with. Not all had paintings displayed in the attic, but many did, especially the important ones, the ones who had made a difference to Moonfell.

"Who was it? Was there a message?" Birdie asked, hands clasping the scarf around her neck.

"No message, but she looked busy. Furtive, perhaps. I think I know who it was." Odette considered the light blonde hair, the gentle features. "I think it was Sibilla. In fact, considering what we're celebrating, it must be."

"The witch who was gifted Moonfell?"

Odette smiled. "The very same."

"It's a sign! Fancy you seeing that far back."

"You know time has no meaning through the moon gates. It could have been a thousand years ago, and yet I would still see if the gates willed it."

"The gate must be trying to tell you something...or she is."

"Perhaps. But first, let's go to the attic to see if I'm right."

Two

November 1523

Sibilla Selcouth stood at the end of the drive, gazing at the manor, thinking that Baroness Catherine Montague must be joking.

"You can't possibly gift this to me!"

"Of course I can. Well, my husband can." Catherine turned to her, eyes shining. "And he's happy to. You can't possibly understand what pressure we've been under. What a relief the birth of a son has given us."

"I understand only too well, Catherine." She had spent a lot of time with Baroness Montague over the past months, and despite their vast difference in social standing, they had formed a fast friendship.

So much so, that the Baroness had insisted that she call her by her first name.

Catherine started to walk up the long gravel drive, trees and shrubs thick on either side, masking the grounds that lay beyond them. "Honestly, I don't think you do. You have four children, and I know you understand how hard it is for women who can't conceive, or who lose babies, but you will never understand the upper class's need for heirs. The way they look at you when you don't produce them. When your husband argues with his family. When he starts looking at other young women and wondering if he made a mistake marrying me... Oh, he loves me, but he *must* have an heir..." She trailed off, stopping to look at Sibilla. "And you gave us one—after losing child after child, and nearly dying myself." She choked back a sob. "Everything has changed because of you."

Perhaps she was right, Sibilla reflected. *How could she, in her lower-class position, really understand those pressures?* Catherine was in her mid-twenties, ten years younger than Sibilla, with the pressure of high royal society that Sibilla, *thank the Goddess*, had never had to endure. Sibilla now had four children herself, and a husband who was a successful carpenter. They had enough money to sustain them—*just*—thanks to Sibilla's special skills.

Her witchcraft.

Not that the word "witch" was ever mentioned, of course. Sibilla was called a wise woman. Well-respected in the community, especially for her healing and fertility skills. That was what had brought her to the attention of Baroness Montague. A helpful whisper from her lady's maid who knew a woman who might be able to help. After long months of herbs and potions and spells, here they were.

"But even so, Catherine, a house? Not just any house either, but a *manor* house!" She had been following Catherine up the drive, both of them enjoying the brisk winter morning, but now she stopped as the house came fully into view. The sprawling, Gothic building with towers and huge, arched windows demanded her attention. "Look at it!"

Catherine dragged her by the hand up the drive. "I have looked at it, many times. There's something unusual about this place, Sibilla. Uncanny—just like you. James doesn't like it. Says it's odd! He never has. One of his many inheritances, and he barely maintains it. It's such a waste."

It was hard to tell that Catherine had only given birth three months previously. Her figure had come back quickly, and her energy. She glowed as she quickened her pace and Sibilla almost had to run to keep up, as did the two lady's maids who trailed behind them. The carriage was waiting at the foot of the drive.

"That is no reason," Sibilla remonstrated, "to give it to me! It's been in his family for generations."

"James doesn't care. It will save him from having to look after it! And you deserve it."

"But there are other practical things to think of. Like upkeep!" Sibilla was sure that Catherine had never had to worry about money in her life.

"Which is why there is also a gift of gold. From me. I'm not so cruel as to give you a house you can't afford." Catherine stopped on the turning circle in front of the house, looking at the heavy wooden door set within a pillared porch. "This is perfect for you."

"You're giving me more money?" She floundered. "But you've already paid me!"

Catherine smiled. "It wasn't enough. Consider all of this a Christmas present, and an advance payment, too. I want more children,

Sibilla. You must help me." She folded her arms. "You're seeing more and more rich women, aren't you now?"

"Yes, that's true. Thanks to you, again."

"No. Thanks to *you* and your skills. I just spread the word a little. You can't continue to see them in your little cottage. No, that won't do at all."

That was true. Sibilla and her family lived in a small cottage in a nearby hamlet, and they were attracting unwanted attention, even though their rich customers turned up after dark for discretion. No matter how many precautions she took, gossip could and would surely spread. Maintaining her clients' privacy was of the utmost importance. She could certainly do that here.

Still, she hesitated.

"What's wrong?" Catherine asked with a trace of impatience. As a baroness, she wasn't used to anyone questioning her. Despite her youth, she'd been brought up to run a household and manage servants. She tapped her booted foot, hands on her hips.

"Nothing's wrong, but," Sibilla lifted her arms wide and spun around as she took it all in, "it's too much! Too big a gift."

"Never mind, you'll get used to it. I'm not backing down, Sibilla. This is your house now."

Alice and Frances, the two lady's maids, caught up with them. Both were young women who liked to giggle, and Alice's mouth was already twitching into a smile. "You should know better than to argue by now, Sibilla. Accept your fate. The house is yours."

For the next few hours they walked through the enormous house, Catherine pointing out ceiling heights, windows, suggesting decorating, and fabrics. It was far bigger than it appeared from the front, as it stretched back into the capacious gardens. Catherine was in her element, and Sibilla knew she had just become a new project. The house was cold at the moment, but the fireplaces were huge, the rooms well proportioned, and the light streaming in through the tall, arched windows was magnificent.

And yes, Catherine was right. The house was a little uncanny. Nothing sinister, though. It felt gentle, welcoming. And watchful. It had stood empty for too long, and it needed company. Life. Although some rooms were empty, others were filled with furniture, and dust lay thick upon the fabrics at the windows. Despite her initial doubts, Sibilla was excited. Very excited.

This belonged to her.

"Who built this place?" Sibilla asked when they stood in the top floor room of one of the towers. The gardens spread below them like a green eiderdown. Thick hedges and walls formed the boundary, and stands of trees stood within it. There were traces of formal gardens, but they had long become overgrown. Bare earth marked some patches. She was itching to explore them. There were also curious archways emerging from the greenery, all around the grounds.

Catherine shrugged her slim shoulders and pulled her cloak firmly around her. "I have no idea. Does it matter?"

"Not really; I'm just curious." She laid a hand on the wall, hoping it would whisper its secrets. "Your husband is right. It does feel a little odd. It has a presence."

Frances, dark-haired, and wide-eyed, took a shuddering breath and stepped closer to Alice. "Ghosts?"

Sibilla smiled. "Perhaps, but there are more things than ghosts that walk this earth, Frances. I have always believed that houses absorb the energies of those who lived within them. Their hopes and fears, joy and despair. And violence. Especially violence. Strong emotions leave an imprint on most things. This house has seen many strange things, I think—not bad, just different. Or perhaps it's just the forceful personality of the person who built it."

Frances had always regarded Sibilla with a mixture of suspicion and awe. Her reputation as a wise woman and healer daunted her. Plus, perhaps the fact that Sibilla cared little for convention. She may be married with children, but that was as conventional as she became. She didn't wear the latest fashions, or dress her hair in current styles. Why should she? She lived on the edge of the woods. Her children, three girls and one boy, were witches just like she was. Even her youngest, at eight years old, showed magical skills. Her husband wasn't a witch, but he practised the old ways. Some people feared them, but not many, and that came only from ignorance. From the minute Frances had stepped inside her cottage, she had viewed it through large, wary eyes, her lips t ight.

Sibilla, however, liked Frances, and as she watched her now, she experienced a flash of her future. Her middle-aged husband, who was tight-lipped and joyless. But there were lots of children, and they made Frances happy, even if her husband did not. Sibilla blinked the insight away and smiled at her. "Don't worry, Frances, houses cannot hurt you. There is a way to cleanse them, chase out the ill-will that sometimes resides within walls, and also banish ghosts. I don't think I need to do that here, though. A routine cleansing, perhaps—for a fresh start. For the house and for my family."

Catherine beamed. "So you're warming to the idea?"

"Of course. How couldn't I? It's wonderful." Her future in the house unfolded before her. She would set up her spell room in this tower. The children could all have their own bedrooms, for once. She could also expand her selection of plants and herbs...and who knew what might be growing there already. "You better show me the garden!

Especially those," she said, pointing to the curious structures almost hidden by greenery.

Her boots and the hem of her skirt were sodden by the time they reached the final arched gateway at the rear of the house, but she was too excited to care. The garden had potential. Lots of potential. It would take a lifetime of work to shape it, and it would keep giving, generation after generation. She knew this. Could feel it. This house would always belong to her family—if they looked after it properly. And maybe a spell would make sure of it, too.

However, these archways were something else. The one before her was constructed of worn stone blocks, fitted snugly together, damaged by the elements, and smothered with ivy and moss. Runes were carved into them, some worn almost completely away. They would take time to decipher, but she could do it. Or her children could. *A game, perhaps.*

"The view through them looks different, don't you think?" Alice asked, cocking her head as she peered through the verdant greenery hanging from the curve of the arch, and casting a teasing glance at Frances. "Like Fairyland. I feel like the Fairy Queen could ride past at any moment."

Frances edged back, but Catherine laughed and marched straight through it. "And yet, my dear Alice, I'm still here! Or..." And then she shrieked and ducked to the side, vanishing from sight.

Frances screamed. "Catherine!"

A giggle came from the other side, and Sibella rolled her eyes. It was tempting to cast a spell to make her vanish better than that, but that would be far too naughty, and Frances might never speak to her again. When Catherine reappeared, she had ivy in her hair and mud on her dress. After years of disappointment that had drained her physically and mentally, in which she had become haggard and worried, it was a pleasure to see her so carefree. *She had done that*, Sibella reminded herself, and through Catherine, the Goddess was giving her a gift she couldn't refuse.

The three young women were suddenly seized with mischief, and they all took off across the garden, skirts slapping on the long grass as they shrieked and chased each other. *That was good*. It gave Sibella a few moments of peace. She turned her attention to the gate again.

All of them were old. Perhaps older than the house. She suspected that this one had either been made from stone that had once made another old building, or the gates had been standing somewhere else for years before finally being brought here. They were all beautiful, and carried a quiet power. Sibella knew they were moon gates, named after their shape, made to offer tantalising glimpses of whatever lay beyond. This one resonated with elemental earth. They must have had a purpose for the previous owner, whoever it was—unless, of course, she was seeing something when there was nothing. However, she could repurpose them now, and the garden could grow around the m.

It was only a few weeks until Yule. It was the perfect time to really make the house theirs. They needed to move in—soon.

Three

December 2023

B irdie stood in front of the oil painting of Sibilla Selcouth, the first witch of Moonfell, admiring her forthright gaze, and glad that for the first time in a couple of years she could not only see properly, but could also manage the stairs to the attic.

In the days since the Goddess had restored a few decades of youth and her health, she had explored the house from top to bottom again, delighting in rediscovering favourite rooms and treasures, looking through photos, and poking around the garden and the glass house. In fact, she'd been so excited at her new lease on life, she'd had trouble settling to anything. She had been in the attic only two days before, breathing in the ancestors, and the smell of mothballs and lavender that protected the old clothes in the chests and cupboards. However, she had not paid particular attention to any paintings, until now.

Sibilla was attractive, but not pretty. She had long, blonde hair that lay loose on her shoulders, and pale, white skin. Her chin was upturned, a challenge sparking in her eyes, but there was amusement there, too. She was seated on an ornate garden chair, plants flowering all around her, a moon gate visible in the far right corner. It was high summer by the look of it, the sky a bright blue. Sibilla almost seemed lost amongst the plants. Both hands rested on her lap, a single rose between them. It was a magical painting. The longer Birdie stared at it, the more she felt the picture was drawing her in.

However, that was true of many of the pictures that lined the walls of the enormous attic that spread over the bulk of the house—well, the oldest parts of it, at least. The witches' power seemed to seep into the fabric of the paintings themselves. But it was fair to say that they didn't know as much about Sibilla as they did about some of the witches.

"You're sure it was her?" Birdie repeated.

"How many times?" Odette asked, getting cranky. "Yes. It was a fleeting glimpse, but it was her."

"And she was carrying something?" Morgana asked. She stood to Birdie's left, arms folded, fingers drumming on her forearms.

"Yes, but I couldn't see what."

"The vision suggests it must be important."

Odette heaved out a large sigh. "Not necessarily. Sometimes I see random things that mean nothing at all."

"Or so you think at the time," Birdie reminded her. "Sometimes, it's months later before you realise the relevance. We shouldn't ignore it. I wonder if there's anything in the library on Sibilla. Other than her grimoires, of course."

Morgana clucked. "Good luck with that! That place is groaning with books and papers, lots of them ancient, but whether there is anything from five hundred years ago is another matter entirely."

Birdie had tried to organise the library years before, but had given up before getting very far. They really should get a professional in one day to catalogue everything. "Well, my dear, we must find out. Unless I can contact her, of course."

Odette snorted, a very unbecoming sound from such a gorgeous woman, but then again, Odette never cared to be precious about her looks or behaviour. She was currently wearing old jeans with holes in them, and a huge, oversized jumper smeared with mud. Her gardening attire. "You wish to ask for instructions, Birdie?"

"As if anything is ever that straightforward where the ancestors are concerned." She sighed. "No, I thought perhaps I might get a glimpse too, through scrying." Birdie finally dragged her gaze from the painting, excitement stirring as she addressed her granddaughters. "Describe what you saw again."

"It was a winter scene," Odette said. "Very typical of the season. Snow lay on the ground. The trees were bare. She wore a long dress, dark blue, Medieval in style, and some kind of wrap around her shoulders. A cloak, perhaps?" She frowned as she recalled the scene. "Anyway, she was relatively young, and there was something in her hands. She was frowning as she hurried towards the gate."

Morgana's eyes narrowed. "Towards it? Not passing by?"

"No. Well, I don't think so, anyway. She looked determined. I wish I had seen what was in her hands."

"Was it small or bulky?" Birdie asked.

"Small, because I couldn't see it easily." Odette was clearly annoyed with herself. "It happened so quickly. Perhaps something will come to me later."

Birdie crossed to the chairs and table under one of the long windows and took a seat. The view was of the uneven roof of the house and the east gardens, with a glimpse of the Waxing Moon Gate. "Let's be logical," she said, as Morgana turned her attention to the next painting, while Odette paced. "It was winter, so this time of year, and she was young. Perhaps it was the same time that she was given Moonfell. After all, it is what we're celebrating tomorrow."

"Also logical," Morgana agreed, "but we shouldn't jump to conclusions."

"Of course not." Birdie's mind was racing as she considered the possibilities. "Odette, you always see the truth of things. It's your skill. What's your gut saying?"

"That it was the first year—a glimpse of when she first arrived here." Odette ran her hands through her thick, curly hair, her gaze distant. "Perhaps she was doing a spell on the gates."

"Perhaps it was *the* spell. The big protection and binding spell that we repeat every year," Morgana suggested. "That makes the most sense. It's an echo."

"Or maybe she was just burying a dead bird?" Odette huffed in annoyance. "Or the family cat."

"Or burying treasure," Morgana countered. "Stop being morbid."

"In the winter?" Birdie said, standing up. "I doubt it. I'll speak to Hades right now. It's quicker than scrying. I am eaten up with curiosity."

"Slow down! Are all the Christmas trees dressed?" Morgana asked, stalling her. "Horty will be here by five, and if they're not, she'll get involved, and before we know it, we'll have glitter and tinsel everywhere! Your sister is insane. She'll also be very jealous of your appearance."

Birdie's hand flew to her face to pat her skin again. She couldn't help but smile. It felt wonderful. But then she felt guilty. Her younger sister would be pleased for her, but it would only remind her of her own lost looks. Even worse, Birdie was likely to outlive her younger sister now. Perhaps that was the downside of the Goddess's gift. Something that hadn't struck her until now. It also meant she was much closer now to her children's age—in appearance, at least. She might even outlive them. She plonked back down in the seat as the significance struck her, her limbs as heavy as lead.

Morgana swiftly crossed the room and sat next to her, a hand resting on her arm. "What's the matter?"

However, it was Odette who answered, her voice soft. "Birdie has just realised the flipside of the Goddess's gift. I think it's time for a cup of tea."

Back in her domain, Moonfell's main kitchen, Morgana felt calm and in control as she made a pot of calming tea prepared from several herbs, but mainly lavender. She placed a jar of honey next to the teapot, and set it in the middle of the kitchen table.

Soft, grey light streamed through the huge windows, and the atmosphere was distinctly moody. She spelled a few candles alight to brighten the gloom, grateful that the range was pumping out heat. She exchanged a worried glance with Odette as she joined her and Birdie at the table, and then both studied their grandmother again.

"I must admit," Morgana said gently, "that I hadn't considered any of that, either. How silly that we should have missed such a thing."

"I was so excited at being younger," Birdie said, sniffing and hands shaking as she poured her tea. "What an idiot."

"Let me," Odette said, easing the pot from her grip. "You are not an idiot. It is a great gift, and you were so unwell before. You had barely moved from your room for months, except to go to the tower the other night. You have every right to be pleased. But there are consequences to everything. On a purely selfish level, I was scared that you would die soon, so I am thrilled that you are in such good health now."

Odette was very sweet, Morgana reflected, *under her wise, uncanny ways, and completely right.* "I agree. This house would not be the same without you. I think the positives far outweigh the negatives."

Birdie huffed. "I can't believe you both thought I would die soon!"

"We didn't mean this week! But perhaps over the next year. Come on, Birdie, you know you were ill," Morgana said crossly as she rolled her eyes at Odette.

"Yes, I was, I suppose. I may have even contemplated my own death at one point."

"More than that. You had talked openly about your funeral," Odette reminded her. "Now it's all arranged, and you can forget it for years. There are far more positive aspects to your situation than negatives, one very large one being that when I have children, you'll be alive to see them."

"You're having children?" That perked Birdie up. "With that lovely young Arlo?"

"Hardly, seeing as we've split up."

"Oh, but Morgana is the pack healer again, so you'll be seeing him far more regularly."

Morgana smirked. Arlo was a wolf-shifter and the Storm Moon Pack's second in command. He and Odette had shared an intense affair that ended suddenly a couple of years before, and no one except them knew why. It was all very mysterious, and Morgana had respected her privacy by not prying. However, they still had feelings for each other; that was obvious.

Odette scraped her chair back along the floor. "If you're going to talk about Arlo, I am leaving this conversation."

"Fine. So then tell me who will father your children!" Birdie demanded.

"I don't know! I just know that I will have some in the future. Can we please get off both of these topics and talk about Yule?" Odette checked the time on her phone. "It's nearly lunchtime. I'm starving, and Horty will be arriving in a few hours. Morgana is right about the decorating. We need to seriously spruce the place up for Yule. We're so late this year. It's unforgivable, really. And you need to get cooking," she said, addressing Morgana. "Do you need help?"

"No, thank you." Morgana preferred to cook alone. She was more organised that way. "We'll have lunch, and then you two can sort the house out. We'll follow up on your vision later. It will keep Horty busy." She winked. "We all know a busy Horty is a happy Horty, so let's keep her witchy fingers occupied!"

By the time four o'clock rolled around, Odette and her grandmother had decorated the three Christmas trees placed on Moonfell's ground floor, their main altar in the sitting room was dressed for Yule, and fairy lights and candles were strategically placed everywhere. And Odette meant *everywhere*.

She and Birdie had been busy for hours. Fortunately, the grand proportions of Moonfell suited ostentatiousness. The first Christmas tree was situated in the entrance hall next to the curving staircase. It was draped in lights and had lots of family heirloom decorations on it. Fragile, delicate things that were wrapped in tissue paper in old boxes when not in use. There were baubles from all time periods—Victorian, Edwardian, the war years, as well as more modern ones.

The second tree was in the formal dining room, which had a table that could seat twenty people, and where they would be eating most of their meals over the next few days.

The third Christmas tree was in the living room they all used, but that was really Morgana's on the ground floor, where Odette was now. They each had their own areas of the house for when they needed privacy, peace, and quiet, but generally they always used this one. It was painted dark green, and ornate wallpaper covered in leaves decorated one wall. The tree was next to the window, again festooned in lights, and with the fire burning and candles lit all around the room, it invited Odette to sit and linger over her glass of wine.

The mulled wine was provided by Morgana, who was looking after them while they worked, but Odette certainly didn't have a lot of time to dawdle. She stood at the window, looking out at the already darkening garden where snow was falling. She could just about make out the Waxing Moon Gate, situated on the east of the garden that the living room overlooked. It was made of yew, dense and bushy, the curve of the arch ten feet high. The hedge stretched away on either side, dividing this section of the garden to create different areas. Beyond the Waxing Moon Gate was a formal parterre garden and fountain.

The path towards it curved between shrubs and beds of perennials, many of them skeletons of their summer selves, but just beyond the moon gate, Odette saw a flickering shadow. She frowned. *Was that Hades?*

Grabbing a blanket off the sofa and wrapping it around her shoulders, Odette, mulled wine in hand, slipped out of the patio door to stand on the paved terrace. Immediately the bitter cold nibbled at her fingers and nose, and the pungent scent of damp earth wrapped around her. The garden was still and silent, hushed with expectation. Odette knew better than to keep it waiting.

She walked down the garden path, the gravel crunching beneath her feet, breath fogging the air; she was glad she had the wine to warm her. She aimed for the Waxing Moon Gate that dipped in and out of view as the path wound through the garden, but just when she thought she was nearing it, it vanished again, and she found that she was on a side path, leading to the north side of the garden.

She spoke into the twilight. "I'm trying to reach the moon gate! Let me through!"

But the leaves rustled, closing off the path. Odette considered casting a spell to force it to let her pass, but the garden knew what she needed often better than she herself did. They had all added their own magic to it over the years. Many Moonfell witches were earth witches, and had moulded it to suit their purposes, but she suspected that Sibilla's guiding hand had shaped much of its layout from the earliest days. The others, like Odette, had just enhanced it. If it liked the changes, the garden would comply. When it didn't, nothing would grow to plan. It always usually worked out. The garden was quirky, magical, and confusing, just like the house.

Odette huffed. "Fine! Be like that." She cast a witch-light overhead, and its silvery glow lit the way down the ever-darkening paths. It was almost the longest night, and darkness fell early.

She passed the path that led to the kitchen garden and glass house, crossing courtyards with benches and cast-iron tables and chairs, arbours and statues, and eventually the New Moon Gate was ahead, lying to the north.

It was constructed of blocks of stone, a pleasing mixture of textures and colours bestowed by time, with a circle of black granite representing the new moon resting on the highest curve. Running through it was a bed of gravel, edged with ferns and mosses. On the other side was a fern garden, dense and lush, perfectly suited to the northern aspect of the garden. A small stream ran through it, and Odette could hear it now, chuckling against the stones.

However, she couldn't *see* the fern garden now. In fact, she couldn't quite work out what she was seeing. She stepped closer, hands wrapped around her glass of wine, until she was only a step away from the gate. On the other side, a wavering, golden light was moving towards her, shadows bounding around it, illuminating a row of pines. The glow grew brighter, until finally Sibilla stepped into view carrying a lantern, giggling at something the young child next to her had said.

Odette froze, as if breathing could banish the vision. The girl was under ten, Odette estimated, almost a mirror image of Sibilla, so she presumed it must be her daughter. She was plainly excited as she skipped along, clutching a wooden box. Sibilla was holding a leather-bound book. Others followed them. A man and three other children, two of them teenagers, Odette assumed. There were some animated discussions—directions or instructions, Odette guessed from the gestures and giggles—and then the vision faded, the candlelight disappeared, and the fernery returned to view, shadows now grotesque in t he light.

Odette stepped through the gate and looked back at it, casting another couple of witch-lights above her. *What were they doing here? Was she seeing one of the first gate spells? Or were they doing something else entirely? Why was Sibilla's whole family there?*

The garden's automatic lighting suddenly came on, spotlights banishing the gloom, and she shivered as reality struck her. She needed to speak to the others.

Four

December 1523

S ibilla stood in her new spell room in Montague Hall, still shocked at the fact that this enormous house was actually their home.

They had been living there for two weeks, and she had veered between ecstasy at owning such a place, and feeling overwhelmed at the work that lay before them to prepare it for use. Her husband had the same feelings, and sometimes they danced with glee through the huge rooms, and other times cuddled around the fire together making endless lists.

The house, though, was meant to be hers. It embraced her. Folded around her as if recognising a kindred spirit. It needed love, especially after being empty for so long, and she would give it that—they all would. Fortunately, the house had embraced her whole family, and they had settled within its walls as if they had lived there for years.

However, unlike the cottage that was easy to keep warm, this place demanded a lot of wood to feed its fireplaces. Thank the Goddess for magic. She cast another spell now, warm air circulating around the room, out the door, and down the winding spiral stairs of the tower. She would repeat the spell through the house later, but that was time-consuming. She needed to design a forever spell. Something clever that would keep the house warm in winter and ambient in summer. She'd been mulling it over for a few days, fine-tuning the ingredients and the words, and she was almost done.

Not only that, the house needed to be spelled with protection, and that would require a very big spell. Fortunately, her children would help. They had run wild for days, exploring every nook and cranny of the place. Despite the cold, she often lost them for hours in the garden.

However, Sibilla had lots to distract her.

Catherine had been as good as her word, and they now had a large sum of money to play with. She had commissioned furniture and linen, clothes for the children, and for her and her husband. He was still working as a carpenter, as he was skilled and in-demand. In his spare time, they tackled the vast garden between them, and had already cleared the area around the house. The rest would wait until the weather improved.

At present, though, she was focussing on Yule and their celebrations, and completing her spell room. Except, she couldn't really focus. Her gaze kept being drawn towards the garden, and before she could think it through, she was marching down the spiral stairs towards the rear door of the house where they stored their outdoor clothing.

In a few more minutes, she had thrown a thick cloak around her shoulders, pulled on her boots, and marched around the house on the barely-there paths to the south moon gate at the front of the house. The children must have heard her, because in minutes, the youngest two arrived at her side.

"Where did you two come from?" she asked, eyeing their muddy clothing. They looked like they had been rolling in it.

"We've been exploring," Mathew, her son, explained. At ten years old, he was earnest, eager to impress, especially his father, as well as imposing upon his younger sister his age superiority.

Sibilla laughed. "What have you found?"

"Bees!" her youngest, Beth, announced.

"Really?" Sibilla looked beyond them. "Where?"

"In the orchard!"

The orchard was a mess, and contained lots of different fruit trees, all of which needed pruning, the grass beneath them long and strewn with rotten fruit. She had wandered through it once, but hadn't explored it properly. It would be one of her spring projects, although she suspected she would need a real gardener to help her. "Are you sure? Shouldn't they be sleeping now? It's far too cold for bees."

Beth rolled her eyes. "A bee house! They're sleeping, but we have explained all about who we are and why we're here. It's okay. They like us. They were listening."

Sibilla had taught her children all about bee lore. She had instilled it in them since they were young. If you kept bees, they must be told the business of the house. It was rude and bad luck not to. If the hives could be salvaged, they would have their own honey. "Show me."

The path into the orchard was overgrown, and the long grass whipped at her skirts. The children, however, found their way unerringly into the centre of the grove of trees where three stone hives were almost swamped with grass and ivy. No wonder she hadn't spotted them before. Sibilla circled behind them, seeing a door built into the back of each stone dome. These were beautifully built, and although they needed a thorough cleaning, were perfectly functional. *Their own honey!* She had always wanted to keep bees at the cottage, but had never really found the room.

She smiled at Matt and Beth. "Well done! Are you going to help me look after them?"

"Yes!" Beth said immediately. "I can sing to them."

Sibilla tried not to laugh at her earnest expression. "I'm sure they will love that, but you must be careful! In the summer, this place will be full of bees. You don't want to get stung."

"I won't. They already like me," she proclaimed confidently. "They will look after us *forever*."

"Forever is a long time."

Beth shrugged, eyes wide. "Bees don't lie. They have been here already for *hundreds* of years!"

Beth did drama well. "The house hasn't been here for that long! It was built about a hundred and fifty years ago."

"But *they* have, in their little houses."

Sibilla crouched so that she could speak to her better. Beth was too young to know her own powers yet, but she certainly had some uncanny traits, and communicating with animals on occasion was one of them. Sibilla knew better than to doubt her. "They're actually called hives, but that's very interesting. They were here before the house?"

"Yes, long before. With the trees."

Sibilla gazed around with new insight. *So, the house was built afterwards. Did that mean anything about the person who had built the house? Or who had owned the land before?* Maybe a distant relative of

Baron James Montague, Catherine's husband. Or maybe the family had bought it off someone else. Or perhaps the Montagues had always owned the land, and had leased it to a farmer for years. She must ask Catherine.

Beth was still speaking. "We need to protect the bees and the house."

"I know. I'm working on the spell right now. We should cast it soon, I think. Yule would be perfect!"

"And we'll help?" Mathew asked. He was too familiar with his sister's ways to be unnerved by her strange speeches. Mathew's magic was vague, as yet, but he was going to apprentice with his father as a carpenter, and Sibilla suspected he would be an earth witch. She hoped that when he turned thirteen his magic would trigger properly.

Sibilla nodded to him. "Absolutely."

"We must use the moon gates," Beth added. "The bees said so. Then the house will be with us forever."

There was that word again. "And how long is forever, Beth?" she asked her daughter.

"Thousands of years!"

"That's a long time. Perhaps hundreds?" Although, that was still a very long time to contemplate the house being in their family. However, it seemed the gates that had intrigued her since the day she first visited here were important. "Do either of you know anything about the gates? Do the bees?"

Beth shrugged. "The man who made the house built them. The bees said so. But that's all they said."

Sibilla stood up, knees protesting after crouching in the long, wet grass. "I must introduce myself to the bees, then. Or perhaps you two should do it?"

"Me!" Beth proclaimed.

For the next few minutes, Beth solemnly introduced Sibilla to the bees, and when the ceremony was complete, she took her children's hands. "Come on. Back to the moon gate. You can help decide our spell."

During the walk back, Sibilla contemplated the placement of the gates. Four positioned on all four sides of the house, built of either stone or metal or yew. All aligned to the four points of the compass. *Were they follies, or something more powerful?*

"You know, the bees are right," Sibilla said once they were standing in front of them again. "I think we need to cast a protection spell with these to protect the house. We can weave the appropriate elemental energies into each one, and then connect them together. They will act like a giant web across the property."

"And we must add spells to the boundary," Mathew pointed out, proving he'd been paying attention to his lessons.

"Yes. That's essential."

"Can we have a gate each?" he asked, eyeing up the south gate hopefully.

"To maintain, you mean?"

"Yes." He laid his hand on the woody stems of the honeysuckle that wrapped over the layers of rough, flat stone and slate that made up the gate. This plant would be gorgeous in the summer, and would cast its scent far and wide. "I want this one."

Already thinking of elemental connections, she said, "It's an excellent suggestion, but I think another gate would suit your skills better."

It would be a way to tie her children's future into the house, and that of their descendants. *Forever*, as Beth had said. Sibilla didn't speak as the spell took shape in her mind. Elemental magic, bound to the four compass points, and the elements they were associated with. And yes, performing the ritual at Yule would be the perfect time. *Or would it? Did she need to secure the gates before completing the protection spell?* She had a few days in which to really explore her ideas, and consider the moon's phases, and how that would impact her spells.

Beth broke her thoughts. "We should make a Christmas present, for the other witches in the future."

"Well, that's very sweet of you, but how would that work? Do we set a time? Or do they just uncover it one day?"

"No! It must have a time. Like a Christmas present."

"A *Yule* present," Mathew corrected. "And definitely a time. A thousand years!"

"Good grief!" Sibilla gasped. "That's too far in the future. "We should say a hundred. Maybe two."

Beth huffed and kicked up the leaves on the ground. "Too soon. Five hundred!"

Her children had little appreciation of time, that was certain. "Beth. That's many, many generations from now. It's madness!"

Both children looked at her, pouting, lips tremulous, and Sibilla sighed. "Fine. Five hundred years. But you both better think of a great present, if it's to be that far away!"

And she needed to work out a way to cast such a crazy spell.

Five

December 2023

"Please don't be cross," Birdie said to her younger sister as her jaw fell open in shock. "I can't bear it! You still look gorgeous!"

"I do not, you lying troll!" Horty said angrily. "And I'm not cross. I'm *furious*. Fancy the Goddess gifting you years, and I still look like a haggard old bat!"

Birdie had been expecting tears, but she should have known better. Her younger sister had always been belligerent, and Horty *was* furious. Her gaze raked over Birdie, and for the briefest moment, Birdie wondered if Horty might throw her glass of port over her. She stepped back, just in case. "You do not look haggard. You're robust! Like an oak!"

"Oh, thank you. So now you're comparing me to a tree!" To be fair, Horty was increasingly stout with age, but the tree comparison was meant as a compliment. However, her little sister could be a little prickly, and Birdie could only conclude that distance had dulled her memories of Horty's moods.

Horty had arrived only ten minutes earlier, while Birdie was still upstairs getting changed out of the dusty clothes she had been wearing to do the Christmas decorations. Odette had let Horty in and plied her with port, escorting her into the living room to warm in front of the fire. She had arrived with Giacomo, Horty's twenty-year old grandson. Birdie wasn't sure where he was. Probably in the kitchen with Morgana, avoiding the fireworks.

"You could have warned me!" Horty continued, stepping closer to scrutinise her, and Birdie kept a wary eye on her drink. "Bloody hell! It's incredible."

"See? You wouldn't have believed me, anyway!"

Horty grabbed Birdie's chin with her free hand and lifted it. "Are you sure it won't wear off?"

"I bloody hope it doesn't!"

Horty finally relented with a huff. "Well, you look wonderful. Maybe I should try to exorcise a Fallen Angel. Could you point me in the direction of one?"

"Fortunately, I cannot—and I mean that, for a very good reason. He was insanely strong, and didn't want to leave. It almost killed me actually, Horty," Birdie confessed, sitting at the end of the sofa that was upholstered in black velvet. "I was unconscious for a while. Had very bad dreams, too."

Horty sat next to her and squeezed her hand. "I know you're younger now, but have you really got the mental energy to be dealing with another twenty years or so of battling with dark things and casting spells? It's hard work. I have to limit my spellcasting now to simple stuff. Spells that won't take hours."

"But it's given me new energy! A lease on life that I'd been missing. It's not just my looks!" Birdie decided to change the subject. It was painful to consider her sister's lack of energy, compared to her own. She was, however, certainly wearing it better than Birdie had been. She was six years younger, and her eyesight was fine, although she did have a little arthritis that magic helped to keep at bay. "I'm sure you'll have enough energy to help us renew the house spells though, and celebrate five hundred years of Moonfell."

"I'll manage that, I'm sure."

"And you'll also need to help us solve a mystery. Odette has been having visions through the moon gates."

"All of them?"

"Just two, so far."

"There'll be more, then."

Horty knew the importance of the moon gates, like all of their family members. Horty had grown up at Moonfell too, before moving to the Cotswolds in her twenties after her marriage to Vigo. It was Birdie who had stayed as custodian. Someone in every generation did. Of course, Horty could have stayed at Moonfell with her husband. The place was big enough, but that was never the way it worked out.

The house chose someone, and it had chosen Birdie. She knew it as soon as she turned thirteen. She had woken up, feeling encompassed within its warm embrace. Fortunately, her husband, Cosworth, had been happy to live there, although he had been dead for ten years now. He was obsessed with jazz, which explained the names of their children: Armstrong, Simone, and Ellington. The house was always full of music, and Morgana had inherited his love of jazz and blues. Birdie had never really taken to it, but hearing it now from the kitchen always made her sentimental.

"So," Horty prompted. "What did Odette see?"

Birdie described Odette's visions. "Of course, it could just be related to the first protection spell, but perhaps not. We cast them every year, and haven't had the visions before."

"As far as you know! It could be a generational thing, and happens every hundred or so years."

"But wouldn't it be in the grimoires? Or the old diaries?"

Horty huffed. "Not everyone records things as assiduously as you! I certainly don't. I prefer reading to writing."

That was true, Birdie reflected. She loved to write things down. She had book after book of diaries, and Morgana had inherited that same itch to write.

Horty sipped her port, face wrinkling in concentration. "You've searched the library, I presume? There must be something in there."

"Not yet. I've been sidetracked with Yule preparations. Besides, you're right. Not everyone likes keeping diaries like me. There are big gaps in our long history here."

"However, we have a library that is groaning with books, papers, and documents."

"You know the library better than me. Perhaps we should search this evening."

"I haven't looked in it for years," Horty admitted. "Not properly, anyway." But a spark of intrigue was already brewing in Horty's eyes. "Yule is tomorrow. If there's something going on, we need to get to the bottom of it quickly. Come on. Let's go there now and get a quick start before dinner. And let's top up the port on the way."

Odette had a theory that the visions should proceed in the right order, and seeing as her first vision had started with the Waning Moon Gate in the west, then the garden had nudged her to the New Moon Gate in the north, she must now travel to the Waxing Moon Gate in the east. There was no point delaying.

She donned sturdy boots and wore a thick coat, scarf, and gloves. She had avoided their guests so far, and had left Giacomo, their second-or-something cousin—she could never keep track—with Morgana in the kitchen. The smell of food was delicious, and Odette wanted nothing more than to sit down and drink wine, but the garden called her, and she didn't like being thwarted.

She left the house through one of the many side doors, having told Morgana she was heading into the shower, and making sure her grandmother and great aunt didn't know what she was doing. They would have wanted to come along, and she didn't need help right now. She wanted silence.

This time, the garden did not object. There were many paths that led to the east where the yew hedge and the parterre gardens lay. When the enormous yew hedge came into view, she walked along it to the gate in the centre. It was snowing again, thicker now, adding to the eeriness of the event; it swallowed up the witch-lights, turning them into ghostly orbs. They were distracting, and she turned them off with magic as she progressed, until by the time she reached the gate, it was dark. The Waxing Moon Gate was the largest, the top of the yew easily rising fifteen feet at its full height, and the gate itself was at least six feet thick.

Many creatures lived in the yew hedge. Birds, hedgehogs, insects, and who knew what else. A short distance from it across a paved brick area, set under a deep arbour, was a wrought-iron bench that in summer was filled with deep cushions. It offered a secret place to sit, read, and think. It was the perfect perch to watch for Sibilla.

But the gate made her wait.

Odette slipped into a meditative state while she waited, wrapped in a warming spell as the cold magnified with every passing minute, a ball of flames floating in front of her. The snow continued to fall, swallowing the paths and shrubs, until they completely vanished and the bushes on either side became indistinct lumps. Instead of seeing visions of the past through the moon gate, Odette saw Arlo.

Ever since he had turned up the previous month to ask for Birdie's help, he had been at the forefront of her thoughts. She had seen more of him in the past months than for the entire last two years, because in that time she had avoided him and Storm Moon, the club where Arlo worked and that acted as the pack base. It wasn't hard. He had made his feelings very clear about her, and Maverick Hale, the pack's alpha, detested witches, anyway. However, because of the events in November, Morgana was now the pack's healer again. That meant, no matter how discreet that Morgana was, she knew all about Arlo and what he was up to.

It also didn't help that he looked so damn good. His muscular frame was lithe and fit, his smile was luminous, and his dreads that she had always loved had grown thicker and longer. Unfortunately, his eyes were wary, guarded even when he saw her, and she hated that. Even worse, Odette could have cursed herself for even mentioning children earlier. Now, all she could think about was Arlo as the father of her future children, and that was impossible. Birdie had given her that look though, and so had Morgana. The speculative look that was so unnerving. It signified plotting. Odette did not wish to be caught up in their matchmaking schemes.

Odette, who could usually always see to the truth of things, was in the dark when it came to Arlo. Damn him, and damn her own emotions for betraying her, because it had become very clear to her that she still loved him, and that was pointless. She'd rather suspect his lack of love than have it pointed out to her—*again*. At least then she could fool herself into thinking that there might be a chance. Something silly to daydream over. Although, from the way he'd looked at her sometimes in their previous meetings, he certainly didn't hate her. That was enough for now.

She was so distracted, and the movement beyond the gate was so subtle, that it took Odette a few seconds to realise that something was happening.

Morgana slapped Giacomo's hand as he went to dip a spoon into the stew. "Hands off, Como!"

"I only wanted to try it." He smiled, pleading. "I'm starving!"

Morgana placed a tray of cheeses and crackers on the table, steering him away from the pot on the hob. "Eat those. You're as bad as Lam. You boys have hollow legs."

"We're still growing," he said, pulling out a chair and taking a seat. "Plus it was a long journey. There was a bit of snow earlier that slowed the traffic, and Horty never stopped talking!"

"Horty does like to chat, and she misses you, I'm sure. It's good of you to have picked her up."

He shrugged. "It's fine. She's good to me, and she loves coming here. She would have struggled to get here on her own. She pretty much commanded me to get her, anyway!"

Morgana laughed. That sounded very much like Horty. "Why aren't you with your parents?" Como's mother, Jemima, lived in Sorrento, Italy with her Italian husband, Paolo.

"They're trying to persuade me to join the family business. I am avoiding that discussion. Do I look like someone who likes soft furnishings?" He gestured to his stocky build that made him look like a rugby player.

"No, but what do looks mean when it comes to work? Office workers come in all shapes and sizes."

"I most certainly will not be an office worker, and I couldn't care less what colour cushions go with whatever coloured curtains. That's their business, not mine."

Morgana crossed to the hob and ladled both of them a generous glass of mulled wine. "But they'll miss you!" she said, handing him his glass and sitting again. "It's Christmas."

He shrugged. "They really won't. Plus, I'll be force-fed Panettone, and I hate it. And then Lam told me that he was coming here, so that sounded far more fun."

"When did he tell you that?"

"A couple of days ago."

Morgana sighed. It was so nice that her son told his cousin of his plans before he'd told her. *Typical*.

"In fact," Como continued, as he loaded up a plate with crackers and cheese, "Moonfell is always more fun than anywhere else—or so I gather. I really haven't had a chance to see for myself." He winked at her. "I was wondering if there could be a bed for me here in the future.

You see, I want to develop my magic, and there's no better place than here."

Giacomo, like many of their extended family, was a witch. Sometimes powers skipped generations, but it rarely happened in their family. Sibilla's line was full of powerful witches, with many different types of magic, although it was fair to say that Como's mother did not use her magic a lot, and generally avoided Moonfell at all costs. She resented the fact that Birdie and not Horty was the house's caretaker, despite the fact that she could have lived there at any point.

"I'm not sure that Jemima would like you being here."

"I don't care. Do you?"

"I guess not. You're an adult and can make your own decisions." Como was twenty, just a few months younger than her son. "This house will never turn away a descendant of Sibilla—unless you deserve it, of course."

"Morgana, I would never betray the trust of the house. Or you!"

The house would certainly be noisier with Como about the place, but that wasn't a bad thing. Plus, it was huge, so that helped. "Don't worry, I trust you. And it will be a good thing. Are you still an elemental air witch?"

"Yes, but my skills are shaky. I need help." He raised his index finger and stirred the air, and immediately a light breeze sprang up in the room, a cool rush of air ruffling Morgana's hair, and turning the pages of her kitchen grimoire that lay open on the table. "I'm always worried I'm going to do something random and give myself away in normal society!"

"Your magic needs an outlet. You just need to make sure you give it one on a regular basis. Somewhere private, obviously. You'll use it a lot over the next few days, and I'm happy to help, and Birdie and Odette will, too. And also your grandmother, of course. We should definitely get some practice in before the big spell tomorrow night."

"Thanks." He lowered his hand and the breeze died away. "Tonight, perhaps?"

"Perhaps. We might have a few things we need to do after dinner. While you're here, pick a room. From then on, it's yours."

He raised his glass with a grin. "Brilliant, thank you. So, as far as Sibilla goes, what's happening there?"

She'd already briefly told him about Odette's visions. "Well, we think it's tied up with the big protection spell that we cast every year, but we have no idea why!"

"A mystery? Good, I love them. Where do we start?"

Six

December 1523

There were still three weeks to go before Yule, and Sibilla had decided what to do about the moon gates, even though she had no idea about the Yule gift yet.

She studied the basic map she had made of the house and gardens, and immediately added another scribbled notation by the south moon gate.

Her husband, Rob, was leaning over her shoulder, nuzzling her neck as she worked. "Can you actually read that? It looks like rat paw prints."

"Of course. You're very cheeky."

"I know." He laughed, his warm breath on her cheek. "Then again, I can't read as well as you."

"You need to practise more."

"I know, but I'm busy, especially now I'm making furniture for our new house."

Robert was typical of many people of their time. He could read but couldn't write very well, but to conduct his business, he had passable skills. Sibilla had been taught by her parents, and she was teaching her own children and her husband, but she was unusual. Many women couldn't read or write at all, but witches needed to record their spells, and her grimoire was full of them.

She twisted in his arms to kiss him. He was lithe and strong because of his work, his eyes creased with laughter lines. "You're a good man." She was lucky that he understood her magic and let her practise it. Like her, he was a pagan who followed the old beliefs, and he certainly wasn't scared of her powers, but he did respect them.

He nodded at the map. "Explain it to me." She turned again and he stood next to her, leaning over the plans. "It looks complicated."

"It's certainly one of the biggest spells I will have cast. In fact, I'm wondering if I can manage it on my own. I wish my mother was around to help." She nibbled on her thumbnail as she studied the scribbled spells. Her mother had died a couple of years before from a chronic lung condition that eventually spells and herbs couldn't keep at bay.

"But the children will help?"

"They are desperate to, and it's important. This house will be theirs once we're gone. The house needs to know them, and be bound to them, too."

"You're doing a binding spell?"

"Of sorts." She tried to explain it better. "I'm doing a protection spell that not only covers the house, but the grounds too, and obviously they're big. But the spell needs to recognise those who live here, and our descendants, too. I'll need blood for it."

Rob jerked his head up to look at her. "Blood magic?"

"It's the only way I know to seal it to us. It's not dangerous."

"But you don't like using blood magic."

"I use it when necessary, though." She squeezed his hand. "It's okay. I only need a little blood from everyone, yours included. A pin prick."

"I'm in the spell?"

"You live here! And our children have your blood, too."

He took a deep breath and sighed. "I guess so. I trust you. Why are you marking the moon gates?"

"Because they will anchor the spell. I need a point in the house too, but I haven't worked out where yet."

"And if the moon gates fall down in the future? Or are removed for some reason?"

That was a good question. She straightened up and looked out of the kitchen window, but didn't really see the view. Instead, she saw her descendants who needed to know the spell.

"I need a new grimoire. One that begins with the house."

"You have a grimoire!" He pointed at the scruffy, leatherbound book on the table. "It's full of your spells, and your mother's."

"It's almost full, and it's a scrawly mess. We've both made so many notes and alterations. It makes sense to me, but no one else would understand a thing. Yes," she nodded to herself, "a new grimoire for a new house and its new spells. It needs to be big."

"The spell?"

"The *book*! I need to organise it—soon!" Her mind raced as she considered how she wanted it to look, the feel of the leather, and the design tooled on its surface. She knew exactly who would make it for her. "Over the years, as I perfect the house and the magic we put in it—all of us—I can detail it in the book. Our children and our children's children will all repeat the spell, year after year. They will know the importance of the moon gates, and the house will be soaked in magic." She beamed at her husband. "I can already feel it soaking mine up now."

"Can you?"

"Yes! This house has been empty and unloved for so long, it's eager for a family."

"That's why the baron didn't want to live here. There's a weird feeling in the Gothic bones of this place."

Sibilla looked at him, surprised. "Do you think so?"

"Yes. You're not the only one who feels things! It's just been empty for too long, that's all."

"What do you think of the moon gates?"

He shrugged. "I like them, but I'm not sure what their purpose is, other than being decorative. I dare say there would have been fine views through them when the garden was tended. And will be again soon."

Sibilla studied her map, finger drifting across the paper. "I think that whoever built this, a distant Montague perhaps, was a little fanciful. The house has all sorts of funny little carvings in the stonework, I've noticed, and the gates are aligned to the compass. That means I can align them to the elements. We'll need water in the west. A pond."

"Perhaps whoever it was just liked symmetry, and Gothic houses are made for drama."

"Perhaps, but it suits our purposes perfectly. I must tell the bees."

Robert tucked a stray lock of hair behind her ear. "The bees are asleep."

"They can still hear everything. Beth said so. The bees must stay, too. Their descendants, like ours, will live here forever."

"You have grand plans, my love."

"That's what dreams are made of." She smiled as he kissed her fingers, one by one. "Are you seducing me?"

"I'm trying, if you didn't keep talking about spells."

"Then help me with one more thing, and then you can."

"All right. What do you need?"

"The children want to leave our descendants a Yuletide present for five hundred years from now."

He snorted. "Five hundred! Let me guess. Beth?"

"And Mathew."

"What kind of present could we possibly leave that won't get damaged, or lost?"

"Well, we have a few options. I just need your help to decide."

"My dear wife, you encourage them with such foolishness."

"It's fun!"

"Then let me seduce you first, because otherwise, I can't possibly concentrate."

Two days later, Sibilla gathered the children in front of the fire after their evening meal. "I need all of your help tonight. We are going to repurpose the moon gates by binding them to the elements. Tonight, because it's the waxing moon, we're going to which gate?" She looked at them expectantly.

"The east!" Grace, her eldest at fifteen, said. She was fair, like Sibilla, and blossoming into a young woman, and a fine witch.

"Exactly. That means what element?"

Rose, her second oldest, was aged twelve, dark-haired like her father, and she answered quickly. "Air."

"Exactly. Each gate will align to an element. You, Rose, are an air witch, so you will look after that gate."

Rose drew a sharp intake of breath. "I will?"

"Yes. Is that okay?"

She nodded, eyes wide. Responsibility suited her children, and rewarding them and growing their magic was the way to do that.

Sibilla smiled. "We are going to burn a bundle of herbs to cleanse the space, and the smoke represents air. What herb do you think we will use? Mathew or Beth, do you know?"

Mathew took a brave guess. "Sage?"

"Exactly. And your father has found us something special to mark the wind. We will put it by the gate."

"Is it a bird?" Beth asked. "Or a bee?"

Sibilla smiled. "Those are excellent suggestions, but actually, it shall be a weathervane. It will turn with every breath of wind. Is that okay?"

"Perfect."

"What do you think this is?" She uncovered the leatherbound book that her cloak had been hiding on the table, and with a flick of her wrist, the cover flipped open and the pages turned by an unseen hand.

Grace huffed. "A book?" She was no stranger to sarcasm when things didn't go her way. Sibilla presumed she was annoyed that Rose had been gifted the east gate. *Typical fire witch.*

"What kind of book?"

"An empty one."

Sibilla sighed. They had been doing so well. "Not entirely." She turned the pages to the first one that was covered in writing. "What might we write in such a big, leatherbound book?"

"Spells!" Beth proclaimed loudly, looking at the book as if it would sprout wings.

"Exactly. It is our new family grimoire. All of you will use it, and when your writing is good enough to be deciphered, you will write in it. For now, only Grace can write in it."

That cheered Grace up. She started to preen. "What gate will I get?"

"What direction is fire aligned with?"

"South."

"Exactly. You will look after the south gate. But we will discuss that another time. Tonight, we will perform the spell, and tomorrow we will all sign the front of the grimoire. It's not just my book anymore. It's ours. Understand?" She eyed them each in turn as they nodded, excited.

Sibilla had written the spell in her own book first, while waiting for the new one to arrive, but had transferred it over that afternoon, feeling it should be written in their new book if they were to cast it that night. It was auspicious. A waxing moon to signify growth, prosperity, and learning.

Perfect.

When they arrived at the east gate, with the first quarter of the moon poking out from behind the thick clouds that had threatened rain all day, Rob was already waiting for them.

Torches blazing with flames and lanterns filled with candles circled either side of the gate that was made from yew trees. The arch of the gate stretched about ten feet high, the inner arch just skimming Rob's head. It formed a hedge that ran to either side, connecting to a low stone wall to encompass the garden beyond. Sibilla had already decided to plant more yews to section off a larger area of the garden, and it needed to be clipped. Years of neglect meant it was growing out of shape, and that afternoon they had already clipped some of the branches back to allow them to pass easily under the arch.

In this light, it was magical. Rob stood on the other side, hands gripping the long, iron pole with the weathervane on top. He had already hammered it deep into the earth to the left of the gate, but it was so tall that it was visible from a distance. It was a very special weathervane with a quarter moon in the centre of the four directional arms.

He smiled at them, ruffling Beth's hair as she ran to his side. "All of my witches together for a little spell-making. I think the garden approves."

"I think it does, too," Sibilla said softly, as the children chattered excitedly. Only Rose was silent as she glided to her side. She was almost as tall as Sibilla. She would have her father's height, as well as his colouring. "Are you ready, Rose?"

"I'm nervous."

"There's nothing to be nervous about. Have you learnt the words?" She nodded. "What if I forget them?"

"You won't, and I'm here to help. Your father can hold the book, so you can see it, if you like?"

"Yes, please. This will be my first big spell."

"And you will do it perfectly. Just remember everything we've talked about. Intention is everything. We are just aligning this gate with elemental air. It's actually very simple. We'll join in once you've started." Sibilla extracted the sage bundle from her pocket. "Use this while you recite the spell."

"How will I know it has worked?"

"You'll see and feel it. Now, you need to light the herbs—use your magic."

Rose looked eager, her eyes wide and nervous, but Sibilla could already feel her power. She would be a calm witch. Centred—just like her father. Rose held the bundle up and uttered the word to command fire, and instantly a flame kindled at one end. She let the end catch fully and then blew it out, smoke spiralling into the still night air.

Sibilla swelled with pride for her young witch as she took her hand. "Well done. Now, let's begin."

Sibilla raised her voice to call her children, and they gathered in a circle beneath the gate, each holding a candle, with Rob holding the grimoire open in the centre. When they had all fallen silent, Rose began the spell.

They all joined in, and as their voices rose, the air trembled around them, making the flames flicker and the grass shiver. Sibilla lifted her candle, and they all did the same, raising their voices and faces to the sky. Clouds vanished, leaving the silvery sliver of moon visible against the blackness. As they chanted the spell, it seemed to grow bigger, until it encompassed all of Sibilla's vision.

She felt the spell's effects rather than saw them, at first. The wind gathered, buffeting them so that her cloak flapped and her hair lifted. *It was time.* Sibilla nodded at Rose, who'd been glancing at her for instructions, and Rose ended the spell, giving thanks to the great Goddess and the moon for their blessing.

A final flush of wind gusted around the candles and torchlight, and then died away completely. Silence fell, interrupted only by the spinning weathervane, winking in the weak moonlight, and a deep feeling of peace sank into Sibilla's very being.

"Is it done?" Rose asked. "Did I do it right?"

Sibilla smiled. "What do you think? The weathervane is still spinning. You did it perfectly."

Seven

December 2023

B irdie cast a spell to turn the lights on in the library, and lit the logs stacked in the fireplace with a click of her fingers.

The library was on the first floor, situated in a long room that overlooked the original inner courtyard. The lamplight illuminated the bookshelves that ran along three walls, the fourth being taken up by several, enormous arched Gothic stone windows with the chimney breast in the middle. The curtains were still open, allowing them to see the snow falling outside.

"It will be a white Yule," Birdie observed. "We'll have to clear the gates if this keeps up."

"By magic, obviously," Horty said, eyebrows shooting up. "I haven't used a spade for over ten years."

"Me neither, but I feel I'm missing out. I used to enjoy digging in the garden, the feel of earth beneath my nails."

"Well, I daresay you can again, with your newfound youth!"

Horty was still smarting. *Obviously.*

"I'm sixty-something, not twenty!" Birdie changed the subject as she watched her sister take in the room. "I always think I made a good job of tidying this place up, and then when I come back in, I realise that I did a terrible job."

Three round tables were placed down the centre of the room, and another couple more were positioned under the large windows. All were covered with books and papers. A set of wooden spiral stairs were situated at each end of the room, leading to an upper gallery where their oldest books were kept. She hadn't been up there in years.

"I don't think anything has changed since the last time I was here at Litha," Horty said crossly.

"That's not true. The cleaners come in, and I know Morgana and Odette use it. You exaggerate."

"I do not."

"You can't possibly know what books were on the tables then—not all of them. Morgana has been in here hunting out old recipes, so I know things are different."

Horty stalked over to the closest table to examine the books. "These aren't cookbooks. They're about gardening—specifically, Elizabethan knot gardens."

"That will be Odette. Maybe Ellington. He was here the other month. He has a client who wanted a knot garden." Her youngest son, Ellington, was a landscape gardener, and Odette had inherited her love of gardening from him. He often used their extensive historical records for his business.

"Well, that's all very well," Horty said, tutting, "but what about cataloguing this place properly?"

"Do we really need to, though? A spell will normally send us in the right direction, and all the really old books are upstairs."

"But having themes grouped together makes much more sense! Look!" Horty stood in the middle of the room, hands open in front of her like a book, and with her commanding voice, cast a spell to find private journals.

Little sparks of light fizzed up and whirled around the room, and in seconds, well over a dozen places were illuminated, as if by fireflies. "See! Why are they in so many places?"

"I don't know. I presume they are logically filed by *someone*! If you're that determined, why don't you sort it all out?"

"Because you very well know that it would take months, if not years! And you've clearly got more of them left than me right now," she added, lips pursing into a thin line.

"I do not intend to spend them in here!" Birdie shot back. She took a deep breath. Anger would not do. The trouble was, she and Horty were both so different. They always clashed. Horty was hot-headed, and Birdie was the complete opposite. "We haven't got long until dinner. Where shall we start?"

Horty banished her previous spell and stood, hands on hips, tapping her leather-clad foot. "If Odette is seeing visions from such an early part of our family's history, it makes sense to look at the first grimoire."

"We keep it locked up now, wrapped in protection spells to preserve it. The yearly renewal spells are kept in a separate book."

"I'm well aware of that. But what if there are incidental notes that weren't transcribed? They might have significance."

"It's possible, I guess." Birdie crossed to the closest spiral staircase. "We can have a quick look."

"Wait. We should look at garden plans, too. They must be here somewhere."

"Really? I've always presumed it evolved over time—well, parts of it, at least."

"But not the moon gates. We know because of the protection spell." Before Birdie could stop her, Horty once again opened her hands like a book and cast another spell to find anything written by Sibilla. Another half a dozen golden lights exploded from her palms and shot around the room. Most headed to the upper storey, but a couple bobbed to the shelves halfway down the room.

They headed to the spot and found a collection of leather tubes wedged into the bookshelves. "Looks like maps," Birdie said, extricating two that were marked by the lights.

The stack was precarious, and although she took her time, a collection of papers and tubes rolled to the floor. Vowing to return to tidy them later, she carried the two they needed to the closest table. "One for you," she said, handing a tube to Horty.

Horty smiled. "It already feels like Christmas. Mmm, vanilla and old paper. Delicious."

An image of Horty as a child, wearing her nightdress and dressing gown, running down the huge staircase filled Birdie's mind. Her sister used to virtually camp out on the landing until the clock struck six, and that was her signal to wake everyone up. Horty had always loved Christmas.

"I think this is a sketch," Birdie said, unrolling the thick paper carefully. "It's a drawing of Sibilla. It's big, too. It's like another version of the painting that hangs in the attic." Sibilla was sitting in a garden chair again, but at a different angle than before, and there was a different scene of the garden behind her. Beehives, by the look of it.

"Perhaps it was one she didn't like." Horty was busy unrolling her own sheet of paper. "It's the garden! Oh, good grief. There's a mass of barely-legible scrawl on it."

Birdie looked over her shoulder. "It certainly isn't drawn by an artist. Look at the house. It's a higgledy-piggledy block. That has to be one of the earliest garden plans."

But before Horty could comment, a bell tolled through the house. They were being summoned to dinner.

Odette slid into her seat at the dining table in the kitchen, slightly out of breath after running through the garden.

"So sorry." She apologised to Morgana, who was placing the crock pot full of rich beef stew in the centre of the table. "I was delayed by Sibilla."

Birdie was already seated next to Horty, filling up their wine glasses, but she paused mid-pour. "You went on your own. Naughty!"

"I had an idea, and wasn't sure it would work, that's all." Over the previous months, with Birdie so restricted to her rooms, she and Morgana had become used to just getting on with things and telling Birdie afterwards. Now that Birdie was back—*almost*—to her formidable self, Odette knew that she would take more of an interest in the day-to-day life at Moonfell again. But that didn't mean that Odette had to discuss *everything*. "I needed space and time to think things through," she said, taking a big slice of crusty bread from the pile in the centre of the table. She buttered it, waiting for everyone else to serve themselves first. "If I'd have told you, you would have crowded me ."

"So, did it work?" Morgana asked before Birdie could leap in.

"Yes. But I saw something different." Everyone looked at her expectantly. "Sibilla and her family were putting a spell on the Waxing Moon Gate. I saw it all." She sighed, licking butter off her fingers. "It was magical."

"Wow," Como said, grinning. "That's so cool. I wish I could do that."

"You can fly, so you get to do really cool stuff, too! Although, yes, it's a blessing...sometimes. I still have no idea what's going on, though. But I did see something interesting."

"Because clearly," Morgana said, "that wasn't interesting enough."

Odette smiled sheepishly. She was still tingling from the experience. "The weathervane that sits on the roof used to be beside the moon gate."

"Really?" Horty asked. "Why and who has moved it?"

"Maybe the hedge became too big. Perhaps it kept falling over?" Odette shrugged. 'I don't know."

"Maybe it's significant," Como said, passing her the ladle. "Like you said, timing is everything."

Odette's stomach growled as she inhaled the delicious scents. She was far hungrier than she had realised. "Perhaps. I don't know how we're supposed to work out what, though."

"It's a series of clues, obviously, and you won't know until you've seen everything," Horty suggested. "Well, that's my theory, anyway."

That was the trouble, Odette realised. *Everyone had theories, and time was short.* She was letting it cloud her judgement. She took a breath and let her worries go. "It will all become clear, and we shouldn't let whatever's happening disrupt our plans. What can I do to help us for tomorrow?"

"Well, I will lead the spell," Birdie said, which wasn't surprising. As the head of the Moonfell Coven, she always led the big house spells, but over the last couple of years, Morgana had taken over. Another change now that Birdie was strong again. Morgana didn't seem to mind. She just nodded. "As to the rest," Birdie went on, a little, impish smile breaking free, "I thought we should mix things up and do different gates. Draw straws, perhaps."

The yearly renewal of their house's protection spells was undertaken by whoever was around at the time. Odette, Morgana, and Birdie, as the three main residents, were always present, and Odette and Morgana's roles were usually always the same. However, it depended on who else turned up. Horty was a regular.

"Draw straws!" Horty huffed and almost choked on her stew. "What on Earth makes you say that? We should stick to our strengths!"

"We all have varied strengths. We should exercise those least used," Birdie said, throwing her shoulders back as if preparing for a fight. "This is Como and Lam's first attendance for a very long time. Maybe ever?" She frowned at Como.

"Ever!" he confirmed. "I've always been stuck with my parents. Not anymore. I'm moving in."

"Moving in?" Horty froze, fork in the air. "When?"

"I'm not sure. Soon. I was thinking the summer, but I could manage earlier. Morgana says it's fine." He shot an anxious look at Odette. "Is it?"

"Of course! Young blood. How fantastic. The house will love it. No family member is ever turned away from Moonfell unless they have seriously transgressed."

"Does that mean someone has?" Como asked, leaning forward, ready for gossip.

"Not for a very long time. That tale is for another time." Birdie delicately probed her stew with her fork. "Seeing as you're an air witch, Como, you should work by the Waxing Moon Gate, in the east."

"Where I was," Odette told him. "Someone will be with you, so don't worry."

"But what does that mean?" he asked, waving his spoon around and threatening all with splashes of gravy. "I'm a complete noob, remember."

"Don't you ever listen to me?" Horty remonstrated. "And lower your spoon. This isn't Hogwarts."

"It's all right," Birdie said. "This place, especially at this time of year, can feel overwhelming. The Yule spell is basically a huge protection spell, the first big one that Sibilla cast on the house not long after moving in. She recorded it in the new family grimoire, almost the first spell put in there—now in the library—and it has been repeated every year since, with some alterations and amendments."

"But what does it do?"

"Protects the house, what else?" Horty rolled her eyes.

"I know that, Gran, but *how*? To do it every year must have significance."

Odette tried not to laugh. Their journey in the car must have been hilarious. Yet despite their short-tempered back and forth, it was clear that Horty loved her grandson, and he was very fond of her. Adored would probably be a word too far.

"It's the scale of it," Morgana explained. "The house and grounds are large, and Sibilla wanted to ensure her family's safety in it. She had four children, all young. This house was a great gift that she did not want to squander. She wanted to ensure that it was handed down generation after generation, and that if someone messed up, the house wouldn't be lost. Witches are not averse to gambling or stupidity, after all, or greed and dark magic. So, she wisely took steps at the very beginning to not only protect the house, but also to secure it to our bloodline. Obviously, the details of its conception have been lost to time, but what has been passed down is the need to do this spell every year."

Birdie continued. "It's tied to the four moon gates and the huge, central staircase—all are anchor points for the spell. In fact," she tapped her lips thoughtfully, "we should add blood magic this year, just like Sibilla did that first year. We haven't done that for a while...not since Lam's birth, and certainly never with you, Como."

"You want my *blood*?"

"A pin prick only," Odette assured him.

"Isn't that dangerous?"

"No. Not for purposes such as these." Odette couldn't resist adding, trying not to smirk, "As long as your intentions with living here are pure, of course. Otherwise, the consequences could be severe."

"Of course they are! I'm not trying to steal it or anything!"

"Then you'll be fine."

"What, er, might the consequences be, if my intentions were dodgy?"

Odette loved to tease. That's why she liked to hide and open the front door by magic, and also use shadow spells in the house on their unsuspecting visitors sometimes. That was the fun part of magic. "Well, people have been known to vanish, somewhere," she lifted her hands, "in the house. The corridors change, as do the garden paths. And the towers sometimes lock themselves for years—sometimes with people in them. Or witches develop rashes that never go away, or their hair falls out. Or they speak only gibberish for months. This place has a way of dealing with people it doesn't like. Best not to test it." She was only half-joking as she recalled the speech issues. *Poor Great-Great Uncle Landow.*

Como looked around the silent table wide-eyed, but no one contradicted her, not even Horty.

"Best you know what to expect," Morgana said, patting him on the arm. "Forewarned is forearmed. I'm sure, however, that you will be fine."

He cleared his throat and reached for his glass of wine. "Okay. So, there are witches on the gates and the staircase, a little blood magic, anything else?"

"A bonfire," Odette said.

"Candles and salt circles," Horty put in.

"Libations," Morgana added, raising her glass.

Birdie smiled. "And it all happens at midnight, of course. We do embrace the witching hour here."

Eight

December 1523

Sibilla watched Catherine study her grand reception room, nodding with approval. Thick, decorative curtains hung at the windows, and Sibilla had placed her best furniture in there. A mix of dried herbs in bowls made the room smell sweet.

"It's already different here. I feel the change." Catherine cocked her head, fixing Sibilla with a speculative eye. "I knew you would suit this place. It's odd, isn't it, the way places speak to us? I've always felt at odds with this house, even though I like it well enough." She laughed. "I think your uncanny ways are rubbing off on me, saying such things."

"There's nothing uncanny about feeling attuned to a house or a place," Sibilla said. "It's about trusting our intuition. It tells us lots of things...you just need to listen."

"Women's intuition." Catherine moved around the room, fingers stroking the solid wooden furniture, some of which had been made over the years by her husband in his spare time. "When will you be able to receive new customers? I know of a couple of women who would like your help immediately."

"To conceive, I presume?"

Catherine wouldn't meet her eyes. "That, and other things."

Sibilla hesitated, weighing her options before she answered. She had never discussed any of her magic with Catherine. The only thing they talked about was herbs to stabilise pregnancy. She had been careful to present herself as a wise woman and a healer. Local men and women visited her for advice on fertility, injuries, poor crops, sick animals, and other benign things. She had certainly never revealed the true extent of her magic. No matter how grateful her customers were, or how desperate, to risk such exposure would be dangerous. *So what did Catherine know, or think she knew?* The fact that Frances and Alice, her ladies-in-waiting, were outside the room suggested subterfuge.

"I could see them in a few days. I'd like to get the house a little more organised first. But what kind of things, Catherine?"

The baroness fidgeted, her fingers playing with the bag at her belt, her eyes darting around the room. A flush started on her neck and travelled to her cheeks. "Well, one of the issues concerns my cousin, Roberta. She's in love, but well, he doesn't..." she floundered, her words becoming a whisper.

Sibilla took a deep breath, knowing exactly where this was going. "He doesn't love her. It seems you think I could change his mind."

Catherine looked at her plainly. "Can you?"

"I'm skilled with herbs and healing. Why do you think I could do that?"

Catherine looked away again, instead focussing on the bowl of dried rosemary and thyme. She rubbed some of the mix between her fingers and inhaled the scent. "Well, there are rumours that some of your healing has been almost like a miracle. Magical, even."

"Some would argue, what's the difference? Magic and miracles. Perhaps it is divine will."

"I prayed and prayed, and nothing would help me bear a child except you," Catherine said, looking her squarely in the eye. "And you save children who are near death."

"Just with medicine."

"But you use words, too. I see your lips move sometimes when you administer herbs. What is that?"

"A blessing." Sibilla answered calmly, but her heart was beating uncomfortably fast in her chest.

Catherine was getting bolder. "It's more than that. You're special."

She closed the distance between them, taking Sibilla's hands in hers. Catherine was used to getting her own way, and now that she had a child, ensuring her husband's heir, she was becoming more self-assured. Sibilla hoped there was no danger from her. She had gifted her a house, after all. *Was that now to be used as blackmail?*

Sibilla must tread warily. "I have been gifted the ability to heal, but that is just an acute knowledge of herbs. How to grow them and prepare them, dry them, make tinctures, lotions, and balms. What combinations work best to do various things. I have been taught those skills by my parents. If your cousin needs help getting pregnant, or even inducing a miscarriage, I can help." She wouldn't be the first young woman who wanted to get rid of a child that she didn't want. "Making someone fall in love is quite different. It's impossible."

"But she's heartbroken."

Sibilla could, of course, cast many spells that could help, but she wasn't going to tell Catherine that. She had a wild glint in her eye that warned caution. However, Sibilla was particularly averse to love spells. "She will find another who loves her as she deserves."

Catherine tightened her grip on Sibilla's fingers. "She will pay handsomely."

"It matters not. She is asking me to change someone's will. Would you like it if a man came to me and declared his love for you? He needed you desperately, despite the fact that you were married, with a child you adored. Say that such a thing exists, and I made such a thing happen, then you would be a slave to an emotion that is not your own. You would walk out on your husband. Neglect your child. Probably ruin your life. Is that fair? Or is that actually terrifying?"

Catherine took a sharp intake of breath. "I see your point."

"I'm glad to hear it. I could, however, make a herbal drink that would ease your cousin's sorrowful feelings. Help her put them aside. Would that suffice?"

After another long, searching look, Catherine released Sibilla's hands. "If you're sure."

"I am very sure. I could make up something suitable in just a day or so. I could send it to you. Or your cousin could collect it?"

"I'll send Alice to get it."

"Of course."

Catherine was annoyed, and this was her way of showing it. But she still needed another child, which meant she needed Sibilla's help. *This mood would pass*, she hoped. In the meantime, she must move on with the house's protection spells. It wouldn't do for Catherine to suddenly change her mind and ask her husband to take the house back. Though such a thing was surely impossible. Everything had been signed legally.

However, the rich liked to get their own way, and as much as Sibilla liked Catherine, she had to protect herself, too.

Sibilla and her children were smeared with dirt, red-faced, and breathless when Rob found them all by the south gate late that afternoon.

The light was already fading under a cloud-choked sky, but she had been determined to stay out and ready the moon gate for the spell. The stonework had been thick with honeysuckle, the dead wood mixed with the living, the plant strangling itself under its own weight. Weeds grew in the layers of stones that made up the moon gate, and long grass was choking the route beneath it.

However, after a few hours of diligent work, the gate was revealed in all its glory.

"What's prompted this on such a grim day?" Rob said, admiring their work. He looked as sweat-soaked and as tired as they did.

Sibilla edged away for privacy and lowered her voice. "Catherine visited me earlier, and it was a little unnerving." She explained what they'd discussed.

"So, she was threatening you?" Rob asked, a deep line creasing between his eyes.

"No, of course not. Not really. I think I'm being paranoid. But I had the feeling that, well, now that we're here, living in a house that was gifted to us..."

"And that is in our name now," Rob reminded her.

"Yes, but I wondered if she thought that I would be somehow beholden, and willing to do *anything* after such a gift."

Rob gave a dry laugh. "A gift you couldn't actually refuse."

"Exactly. I tried to say no...well, initially. I must admit that after my first reservations, I really wanted it."

"Who wouldn't? But you put her off, earlier?"

"Of course." Sibilla watched the children, slightly distracted. "I'm grateful to her, for her business and referrals, but I'm not stupid. Besides, she needs me if she wants another child. She won't push me too far."

"No. Not immediately, of course. Not until she has a full brood of children. But in a few years, what then?"

"By then, I hope she's so grateful, and that I'm so established, that she wouldn't dream of it. But that's why we need strong protection spells now. This is of course something that we were doing anyway, but I'm bringing forward the gate spells."

The spell on all four moon gates would be tied to the four main moon phases. She had known that she couldn't wait for the whole month to cast the spell on all of them, because she needed to cast the house and family protection spells at Yule. The full moon would be in another few days, and then the waxing quarter moon the week after that. That would mean only one gate needed the full spell after Yule. *But after this morning...*

"You're rushing, and you don't need to." Rob pulled her into his arms. "Can you imagine how people would talk if she were to cast us out of here? Despite all her wealth and position, she would be a pariah."

"She wouldn't care. The rich have different standards to us."

"She won't do it. Like you said, you have time. Besides, say she did decide to throw us out and try to ruin our business. If we had to, we could go anywhere in the country to hide from her—we both have skills. But she needs you too much. She was just trying her luck, and you have made your position clear. Wait until the full moon for this spell. It will be fine."

Rob's calm, wise words did much to ease her fears. Sibilla didn't normally become unnerved so easily, but this house... "This place is already under my skin. I can't bear the thought of losing it—ever."

"Baroness Montague, for all of her youth, is very perceptive, and she knows that. Besides," Rob's gaze shifted to the house, "I have the feeling that the house will not let us go, either. Plus, you have other options."

Sibilla started at his words. "A spell on *her*, you mean?"

"You could bind her to your will. As a last resort, of course."

"I won't do that. I chastised her this very day about love spells, which are almost the same thing."

"I know, but you need to remember that you are not without resources." Rob sighed and changed the conversation. "However, the gates need clearing, so over the next few days, we'll all work together to do it."

By the time the full moon rolled around, Sibilla was feeling calmer.

Alice had visited to collect the herbal tea for Catherine's cousin, and had seemed to be her usual, cheerful self as she passed on Catherine's regards. However, she hadn't lingered, as the carriage was waiting on the drive. She certainly didn't ask questions about love spells, either.

It also seemed that the Goddess was smiling on them that night. The heavy, cloud-laden skies had cleared, and as they set off across the garden, the moon guided their way. It was another late night for the children, but they didn't care. Beth and Mathew had gone to bed as usual, and found it very exciting to be woken up to cast spells at midnight. The oldest two, however, had helped in the preparations.

"Grace, are you ready?" Sibilla asked her eldest as they walked together.

"Yes. I've memorised everything. I'll be fine." Her voice was confident—overly so. At fifteen she was already fiercely independent. "I won't need your help like Rose."

"No, I'm sure not, but I'll be right by your side anyway."

"But you won't interfere?"

Sibilla rolled her eyes. "No! Honestly, Grace. I only ever want to help. I will only step in if you're in trouble. As I know you won't be, then all will be fine."

They were using fire to bind the south gate to the full moon. They would light a fire and cast a circle around it marked by candles. The spell was simple, but intense. Sibilla aimed to bathe the whole gate in fire, but leave the plant untouched. Almost like a sort of rebirth, or a consecration.

While Grace completed her preparations when they reached the gate, Sibilla lit the candles around the circle with a spell. The flames burned clear and steadily, and Sibilla looked up at the moon.

It seemed to her that the whole garden was waiting with bated breath for the spell, as if it knew what was coming. The orchard was a stone's throw away, and the shadows beneath its bare branches were dark and thick; she was sure she could hear the bees murmuring.

She turned to Grace and took a deep breath. "Time to begin."

Nine

December 2023

Morgana left Birdie and Horty on the main floor of the library, and mounted the spiral steps to the mezzanine level, with Como at her side.

After dinner, Odette had insisted on returning to the garden and the next moon gate, feeling that once again she would see a glimpse of the past, and perhaps a reason why she was seeing them at all.

"So, apart from the oldest grimoires, what else is on this level?" Como asked, as he studied the books on the shelves. "They look ancient."

"They are. And expensive, which is why they're behind glass."

"Like how expensive?"

"Like build a new wing to the house expensive."

Como's mouth fell open. "Holy shit, Morgana. Really?"

"Really. There are a few first folios in here, and lots of first editions. Something for a rainy day, if we are in dire need."

"So, not everything is a complete jumble, as good old Granny Horty suggests."

"Oh, down there it is, but up here, we take care to keep things safe. Especially our collection of some very unusual books on the occult and magic."

"Spell books?" Como asked.

"Some are, but not in the conventional sense. There are many Medieval volumes that talk about summoning demons, all written in Latin. One of our ancestors, I forget his name, was obsessed with them. He pretty much bought every book he could find. Practically lived in Burton and Knight, as well as trekked around rare book shops."

Como had been slowly advancing along the shelves, peering in at the contents, but now he paused to ask, "Who are Burton and Knight?"

"It's an auction house in Chelsea that sells occult goods. They've been going a long time, so this was back in the nineteenth century."

"Wow. No wonder everything is behind glass."

"There are a few alchemical volumes, too. European and Middle Eastern in origin. Absolutely fascinating images and weird esoteric passages, but as interested as I am in alchemy, I barely understand a thing. I believe our ancestor had many adventures tracking these down." She stopped in front of the display case that contained them, captivated by the allure of their titles in glorious fonts. *One day*, she promised herself for the hundredth time, *she would study them properly.*

"But these aren't books," Como said, breaking her concentration. He pressed his nose to the glass door of another case, and Morgana crossed to his side.

"Ah, you've found the old tarot sets. Early ones, these, a hundred or so years old. They are a little different to our modern decks. We have some very beautiful designs. Even though they are protected with spells, they are fragile."

Morgana scanned the long shelves stretching away into shadows. It was darker on this level, with soft lighting, and although the cabinets could be lit from within, she chose to keep the light subdued. It was as if the books absorbed all sound, and they could barely hear Horty and Birdie chatting below. It was comforting on the mezzanine, and it was easy to spend hours browsing; as a child, she had curled up on the leather chairs placed in small alcoves, lost in the words for hours. She tried not to now, of course. No one handled the books unless needed, even though they had placed protection spells on them. However, at present, it wasn't rare first editions she was interested in, and with an effort, she focussed on the task at hand.

She walked halfway down the mezzanine and stopped in front of glass-fronted shelves containing very large and ancient leatherbound books. A reading stand was close by, and she took out a book bound in brown leather, surprised as she always was by its weight.

"That's it?" Como asked, helping her lift it onto the stand. "Sibilla's grimoire."

"Sibilla's *Moonfell* Grimoire," Morgana corrected him. "She had others, including her mother's, but she started a new one when she moved in here. Many other generations added to it, of course, including her children. That was how she designed it. A true, family grimoire." She pointed to the many other books in the cabinet. "Elizabeth, her youngest daughter, has a very interesting Book of Shadows. She had an unusual skill, and she documents it in there."

"What skill?" Como asked reaching inside to pick it up.

"She could communicate with animals and insects."

"Like Doctor Dolittle?"

Morgana laughed. "Sort of. It's a rare skill that not many witches have."

"So, not like talking to a familiar."

"Oh, no. It's nothing to do with familiars at all."

Como pursed his lips, the muscles working in his jaw. "My mother never talked about this stuff! All of this is brilliant, but I feel she's hidden so much." He turned the pages of Beth's grimoire, the thick paper seeming to whisper as they flipped. "I'm just itching to read everything! To *discover* everything!"

"It would be a lifetime's study, so I suggest you narrow your aims." Morgana felt sorry for him. Jemima was an odd one for keeping such things a secret. For those who truly belonged to Moonfell, the place would always find a way to bring them home and nurture them. Como was one of those. "You're back now, or will be soon, so maybe pick a topic then, or a timeframe to focus on. Come, this isn't getting us any closer to what the gates might be trying to show us."

Morgana bypassed the list of names at the front of the Moonfell Grimoire and turned to the first spells cast on the moon gates. Sibilla's writing was clear and distinct, but nevertheless, the meaning was difficult to discern easily, and she realised she'd forgotten much of the information contained there.

"Bloody hell, it's like trying to read Shakespeare," Como complained.

"If you're to study old grimoires, you'll have to get used to that. It's surprising, though, how quickly you fall into the rhythm of it. Here she's listed how she linked the gates to the moon's phases. This last one, the New Moon Gate, she did twice, because the first time she had to hurry to complete it for the protection spell. She did it outside of the correct phase. I'd forgotten that."

"Would that have caused problems?"

"Not with the protection spell. Binding the gates to the moon phases was an extra embellishment. An affectation, really, but a fun one. A little magical excitement."

"Why?"

"The gates always look different in their own moon phase. They have a special glow to them." She pointed to a few sentences at the top of the page. "She explains it here. The moon gates were already present in the grounds, and she fell in love with them. She decided they were too good not to repurpose. She wanted to make the house her own."

"Very cool! How does that relate to Odette's visions?"

"Excellent question."

Morgana turned a few pages, admiring the sketches of the gates at the top of each page, the spell and ingredients and rituals inscribed beneath.

"Is there a sequence for the gates?" Como asked, leaning over her shoulder.

"For the protection spell? There used to be, but now we start the spell at each gate simultaneously."

"I should have gone with Odette," Como said, frustrated. "I really want to see the gates now."

"You're not missing anything tonight, because you won't see what Odette will. You can see them tomorrow in the daylight. I certainly don't recommend you go now on your own. Not until the garden is used to you." Morgana tapped the page. "Focus on this. I wonder if revealing spells will show us something."

She cast the one she used most frequently, hoping that unseen writing on the page would be unveiled, but the breath of magic across the page achieved nothing.

"Let me," Como offered.

For the next several minutes they each tried a variety of spells, until finally a shimmer of light flashed across the Yuletide spell, and letters hovered in the air, along with the tinkling of bells. Morgana gasped with delight, but her excitement quickly vanished.

"That minx!"

Como was exasperated. "What did it say? I couldn't read it!"

"*Wrapped in spells with Yuletide bells, a gift from me to you, but you can't cheat, the clock will know, and only Yule will do.*"

Como's face wrinkled with confusion. "Which means *what*?"

Morgana bubbled with excitement. "Something different must be happening. Odette is right! However, we're a day too soon, but one step closer to whatever Sibilla has planned!"

"But that verse could be meant for any year," he pointed out. "Not necessarily this year."

"The gates don't lie, Como. It's this year. I'd stake my life on it."

Odette waited at the Full Moon Gate to the south of the house, full of anticipation.

However, the snow was getting thicker by the minute, and the temperature was plummeting. She sniffed the air, lifting her face to the sky so that snowflakes settled on her cheeks and eyelashes. *This snow isn't normal.* The knowledge struck her so suddenly that it felt like an icy slap. It was too cold, too intense, too...*other*.

Odette turned to the south, expecting to see something, but other than a thick curtain of snow, she saw nothing at all. It wasn't intended for them, though, whatever mischief it contained. It was heading southwest. An uneasy feeling settled in the pit of her stomach. It carried threats, not just mischief, but there was nothing she could do about it. She only hoped whoever it was intended for could deal with i t.

With a dissatisfied shrug, she turned back to the moon gate, muttering under her breath. "I'm waiting, Sibilla. Garden! Can you hear me? If you have something to say, spit it out!"

She should have known better. It was impossible to rush these things, and as the minutes stretched on, she became colder and colder, despite her warming spells and thick jacket. She was dimly aware of the rumble of a car engine and headlights cutting through the snow, and realising that someone had arrived, she cut her losses and headed to the drive.

The sleek, silver car had pulled up in front of the main door, rather than circle around the back of the house to the old stables, of which part had been converted to garages. She frowned as she recognised the car. It was her father's, and she hadn't been expecting him until the morning. However, as three doors opened and its occupants spilled out, she realised that actually everyone had arrived at once—Uncle Armstrong, Lamorak, and her father, Ellington.

She shouted in greeting as she emerged from the path by the hedge. "Hello! We didn't expect you until tomorrow!"

Uncle Armstrong, Morgana's father, waved first, unencumbered by bags, unlike Lamorak, Morgana's son, who was already lifting luggage from the boot of the car and looking pensive. Her father swiftly crossed to her side and hugged her. "What are you doing out in this weather? You look half frozen."

"I look worse than I feel, don't worry."

Her father might be sixty, but was still a handsome man, with a head full of thick, grey hair. His brown eyes, always so perceptive, peered deep into her own. "You were on a mission! What's going on here?"

"I'll tell you inside. It's far too cold out here. Why are you all here now instead of tomorrow?" she asked, as they joined the others by the Jaguar.

"The bloody weather," Uncle Armstrong said. "As soon as it started snowing this morning, I knew it would only get worse. I rallied the troops. Couldn't let Moonfell down at Yule. Besides, I wanted to see my daughter and grandson." He beamed at Lamorak, who rolled his eyes. *Typical teenager.* Armstrong just laughed. "Thanks Lam, always a joy." Armstrong was close to seventy and hadn't aged as well as Ellington. His hair was thinning, and his broad shoulders were rounded, but he was always relentlessly jolly, unlike Morgana, who had a streak of seriousness at all times. He was dark-haired like her, although his was iron grey now.

"And how are you, Lam?" Odette asked, helping to lift bags of food out of the car.

"Wondering what I've signed up for, actually, with this Yuletide malarkey," he said, walking up the steps to the front door. Lam was tall and rangy with a long stride, and Odette had to hurry to keep up.

"Hardly a malarkey, protecting your ancestral home," she shot back. "Anyone would think you're staying until the new year with all this food. Are you?" she asked, as an afterthought.

"No. I have exams and revision to do...and things." He was purposefully vague, and she wondered if he had a girlfriend—or a boyfriend, perhaps. Or maybe he was just protecting his privacy. He didn't often come to Moonfell, and therefore didn't know Odette that well. Plus, like many people who were unfamiliar with the house, he found it overwhelming; that much was obvious—to her, at least. Although, he was trying very hard to hide that.

Odette spelled the front door open, and as they entered the imposing hall, shouted, "Guess who's here?"

But the only response was silence.

"They're all up in the library and can't hear us," Odette told them as they shook snow off their coats and stamped their feet on the mat. "Make yourself at home; you have your usual rooms. I'll fix you drinks, and then we'll join the others."

Birdie lifted her chin, eyes defiant, as she met the shocked stare of her two sons. "I like the new me!"

"It's actually the old you," Ellington pointed out, eyes narrowed. "From twenty years ago, actually. Good grief. It's incredible."

Armstrong looked pale. "But you look *our* age! It's just not..." he hesitated. "I mean, it's fantastic, it will just take a little getting used to." He stepped closer, and Birdie was sure that if he'd had a magnifying glass, he would have whipped it out to examine her more closely. "Do you feel different, too?"

"Yes! Twenty years different. I don't ache as much, and I can see again. Aren't you happy for me?"

"Mother, dear," Armstrong kissed her cheek, bending down to do so, "of course. Like I said, it's a shock, but you really do look wonderful."

"Thank you. It's lovely to have you home."

He wagged his finger, admonishing her. "You obviously did a very dangerous spell."

"Very successfully," Morgana said drily as she raised her glass. "We banished one of the Fallen. I think we should be drinking champagne."

They were all in the library, crowded around the table that had the garden plans spread over them, except for Lamorak and Como, who had abandoned them to talk by the fire.

"Darling." Armstrong hugged his daughter and kissed her cheek. "I didn't mean to doubt you."

"I should hope not. We are the guardians of Moonfell, after all, and have to deal with anything that lands on our doorstep. That includes the Fallen, and Nephilim, and shifters, for that matter. It's been a busy few weeks." She rolled her eyes at Odette and Birdie, and both sniggered. "How have we managed without men here?"

"Quite so," Horty said, leaping to their defence.

Ellington winced. "Ouch! I think you deserved that, Armie."

"Thanks, *Ellie*," he said, calling him by the name he detested.

As much as Birdie loved seeing her children, she also loved to see them leave again. They disturbed their usual habits, and her two sons were infuriatingly sexist—although they never saw it in themselves. She would train Como better, and Lam, if given half a chance.

"So," Ellington said, swiftly changing the subject. "Why the plans? Are we having a treasure hunt?"

"Well, funny you should say that," Odette began. "I've had some interesting visions of our ancestor Sibilla's past activities, and I think something is going to happen this year. No," she corrected herself. " I *know* something will happen. It's the five-hundredth year of us inhabiting Moonfell. A milestone. We want to find out what it could be."

Ellington was sitting in a chair, manspreading his legs wide as he surveyed the table, as if he was master of his domain. It irked Birdie no end. Her youngest son always had a way of imposing himself on everything. *At least he knew better than to question his daughter's instincts.* "And you're looking for clues," he said, nodding sagely.

"We thought the original plans would be a good place to search," Horty said, "but there's just a lot of notes and nothing in the slightest that helps us."

"Yet," Birdie agreed.

"Unfortunately," Morgana said, looking a little smug, finger winding in her long hair, "We won't find out until tomorrow. I've just found something in the Moonfell Grimoire. Sibilla left a message."

"How?" Birdie asked, annoyed that she'd been waylaid by Horty and the garden plans.

"A hidden message I only found with a revealing spell. Como helped me discover it. It was playful. A tease. '*Wrapped in spells with Yuletide bells, a gift from me to you, but you can't cheat, the clock will know, and only Yule will do.*' Fun, isn't it? And," she added, smiling at Odette, "it means that you were absolutely right. Again!"

Birdie felt horribly disappointed not to have seen the message, but at least it confirmed everything they suspected. The next day's preparations would have an extra fizz, and she needed to throw more of a party.

Ten

December 1523

"I know what I want to do for a Yuletide gift," Sibilla said to Rob late one evening after the children had gone to bed. "But I need your help."

They were in their sitting room, and Sibilla was working on the house protection spell in her new grimoire. There was only a week to go until Yule, and she had begun to panic about the self-imposed gift.

Rob was tending the fire, a goblet of wine in his hand, and he looked at her, amused. "I knew I would be roped into this. Go on."

Sibilla set her quill down, careful not to splash ink. "This house will change over the years, possibly a lot. There might be new wings or outbuildings, and the decorating will certainly change as fashion does. However, as I've mentioned, I've decided to base my spell on the four moon gates and the central staircase. The staircase is unlikely to ever change. I suppose the main room configurations won't change either, but it's so hard to know for sure. I think it would be lovely to gift our ancestors a copy of how the house is now. We could give them a wooden carving of it, and I could hide it somewhere in the staircase."

Rob gasped. "You want a carving of the entire house? In *one week*? I'm a good carpenter, but not a miracle worker."

"Only a small one," she hurriedly explained. "A miniature, just of the outside. Well, maybe with the inner courtyard, too. And maybe," she added, excitedly expanding on her original plan, "we could make a bigger one and leave a clue to it in the smaller one."

"So now I'm making *two* houses?" He laughed and brushed his hair off his face. "Is that supposed to help me?"

"The second one could take months, so you can take your time over it. All I need in one week is a tiny little house as a gift." Her fingers drummed the table, and she stared at the fire as she planned her spell. "A wooden house that details the windows and the doors, and I could spell it to make something magical happen. I just need a trigger."

Rob joined her at the table, reaching for the quill and a sheet of paper. "I am obviously very easily led—well, by you at least—because I actually think that is a fine gift. I can work on it in my spare hours, in the evening." He held his hands apart. "I could make it this big. I have plenty of wood to choose from. Which, I suppose, brings me to my own request."

Sibilla smiled at him, wondering how she could be so lucky to have found such a man. "You hardly ever ask for anything."

"That's generally because I want for nothing." He leaned forward and kissed her. "But seeing as we have so much house now, I would like a room to work in. A sort of studio. A workshop. I've been looking at the stables, and I could section off some of it. It will need clearing out and tidying up, of course. What do you think?"

"I think it sounds perfect, but you could have a room in the house, if you want."

"I would be too loud, and I would trail wood and sawdust everywhere. Besides, I need man space," he said, a twinkle in his eye. "It would mean I could make bespoke items too, and perhaps eventually I could even set up on my own, rather than work for Adamson."

It had always been a dream of his, but with such a small cottage before, and little money to find his own place, it had been impossible.

"This house keeps on giving, doesn't it?" she said, smiling softly and allowing herself to dream. "We have room to grow here."

The reality of being in it was still odd. She had to pinch herself to believe their luck. Or maybe it was fate, and a just reward for her skills. But the minute the thought entered her head, she grew worried again. Losing this house now would crush her. Would crush all of them. In such a short time, her children were already flourishing here, and so was Rob. He looked excited, and he deserved it. Immediately, her thoughts returned to the spell.

"I must get the spell right, Rob. I have to. I feel our future depends on it."

"We'll survive without the house, you know that. We have for years."

"I know, but..."

He kissed her fingers. "I know. You work on your spell. I'll start my sketches. And stop worrying."

On the day before Yule, after all four moon gate spells had been completed, Rob showed Sibilla his carving of the house, and she squealed with excitement.

"It's beautiful!"

"It's good enough," he said, ever critical of his work. "The next one will be better. I've started gathering wood for it, and I've made the base."

"Already?"

"It has fired up my creativity."

Sibilla crossed to the window clutching the small wooden house, eager to see it in the pale winter sunshine. She held it to her eyes, admiring the fine, detailed workmanship. It was the size of her handspan, and was an exact miniature of the house, down to the chimneys, the arched windows, and the doors, and there was even a courtyard in the middle.

"I made it in sections," Rob explained as he took it from her and pointed out the joinery. "This way I could put the windows in the courtyard walls, too. It's made from cedar wood."

"What a brilliant choice. Do you know what properties cedar has?"

"I may have learnt a thing or two from my talented wife. Protection and longevity, and it drives away evil spirits. Am I right?"

"Yes, and it's used for purification, too. A sacred wood."

"Also used in temples," he said, tapping his nose. "I know my wood. Happy?"

"Very."

"You have a spell prepared?"

Sibilla sighed, brushing her hair from her shoulders. "So many spells. With the moon gates now complete, I can focus on this today, and then tomorrow... Well, it's the big one."

"There's a lot of house here to cast a spell on your own."

"The children can help. We'll start outside and then I'll finish at the staircase. It will be fine." She said this with more confidence than she felt. It truly was a big spell, and she wished her mother could help.

"Where will I be?"

"With Mathew, and then Beth, when he's settled. Don't worry, he'll be fine."

"It's not him I'm worried about."

"We can take our time over this spell tomorrow. It will layer up, spell upon spell, place upon place. We can start at one gate, and then move to another. The children are quick to learn, and they've been practising all week. They're so excited. I'll have to strengthen their spells of course, afterwards—at least I think I will, but that's okay. They will sort of..."

"Lay the foundation," her husband said, finishing her sentence.

"Exactly." She turned her attention to the solid wooden house that she once again held, the wood warming beneath her touch. "But this afternoon, we shall put a spell on this."

However, that afternoon, a woman called Matilda, who was of Sibilla's own age with three children, arrived at the house on foot, cheeks flushed from the cold. They were friends, of a sort, and Sibilla took her to the kitchen.

"So, this is Baroness Montague's gift?" Matilda asked, eyes wide as she took it all in. "You know that people are talking."

"I'm sure they are, but there's nothing I can do about that."

Matilda accepted the herbal tea she offered and stood at the window, looking out onto the grounds. "You will lose customers, I think. Some of the peasants and poorer folk won't come to see you here."

"I've considered that. I shall go to them. We'll buy a horse, maybe even a carriage. Something simple. I'll make it work."

"Still, they'll be suspicious."

"Why? I'm still the same. I just happen to have helped Baroness Montague give birth. I do it for everyone. It's my gift."

Matilda, her dark hair curling around her face, smiled. "I know, and you're very generous with it. Poor Jen's youngest is ill. I think she'd like to see you but is too scared to ask. Reckons you won't have time for her."

Sibilla's anger rose, quickly followed by regret. She knew that living in this house would have consequences, but she would work hard to overcome them. "Then I will go to see her now."

"She has already asked Meg."

"Her skills are nothing compared to mine."

"But she's still living in the village, and therefore easy to get to." Matilda sipped her tea. "I'm sorry, but I thought you should know. We haven't seen you in the village for weeks. Someone else has already moved into your cottage."

They had rented the cottage from the local landowner, like many in the village. "That's as it should be. It's a fine house, and someone should use it. And I suppose I don't need the money as much as Meg, but..." Sibilla's voice faded as her guilt settled in. She would do better than Meg, and she was letting people down. There was also the possibility that resentment bred distrust, and that led to gossip. She couldn't afford gossip about her skills. That could be dangerous if the word *witch* was ever mentioned. She needed to keep everyone on her side. "I can find time to visit in the morning, just to say hello to everyone. I need to let them know that I'm still available. Will you tell them that, too?"

Matilda nodded, distracted as she studied the room, clearly in awe, and then she said the same thing that Catherine had. "It suits you. This place, I mean."

"So I've been told. The children love it here. So does Rob."

"And all this land! You should get sheep. Or goats."

"Maybe I should, but they just take time to look after, and I will be working."

"With a few fine folks, I presume?" Matilda kept her tone light, but she was clearly suspicious of Sibilla's promises. *Perhaps she was right to be.* Life changed, that was a certainty, but Sibilla meant every word. She would try to help the villagers as much as they would let her. She would prove them all wrong.

"With everyone," Sibilla insisted.

Matilda was right, in one respect. She had been so caught up with the move that she had neglected them—all of her old friends and neighbours. That would change. Despite being busy with the protection spell, she would visit the village the next morning.

Eleven

December 2023

Birdie woke with the dawn and lay in bed, breathing in the silent house. This was probably the most peace and quiet she would get all day.

With the arrival of their guests, already the energy of Moonfell had changed. Fortunately, Ellington and Armstrong had participated in the Yule spell often enough to know their parts—although, as she had said to Horty the day before, she wanted to shake things up a bit. Maybe it was to do with her own shake-up that was imposed on her by the Goddess.

It was strange to think that five hundred years ago on this very day, Sibilla had rallied her children and cast the spell to tie Moonfell to their family forever. A few months ago, Birdie had just been content to let their Yuletide celebrations and the annual spell unfold, but not anymore. Sibilla had left them a gift, and she wanted to make a grand gesture, too. Something dramatic, and also fun. Something that would help Lam and Como feel more at home. They were young and needed to appreciate the fun in witchcraft, as well as the mystery of it. They would see both today.

She had been inclined in recent years to see the Yuletide renewal spells as a necessary chore, because really, she doubted anything could take Moonfell away from them now. However, old age and impending death had made her aware that nothing was forever. Moonfell must endure, and today's spell would continue that tradition. But change was important, too. So yes, there would be fun on the longest night of the year, and that meant she wanted something to light up the darkness.

Eager to get on with the day, she slipped out of bed, shivering as she pulled on her thick dressing gown and padded to the window. She gasped with surprise as she pulled back the curtains; she had expected to see snow, but not quite this much.

The garden had vanished under several feet of snow. Tree branches were bowed beneath the weight of it, and the unusual topiary had taken on grotesque shapes that suggested monsters lurked in the garden. Birdie's room overlooked the rear of the house, and the north gate was just visible, but again, that was covered in snow. Everything looked pristine. Hades was probably still out there. The weather never bothered him, but often when it was this cold, he would lie by her bed at night. He wasn't there now, though.

Birdie stilled her mind and closed her eyes, and in moments she was with him, seeing through his eyes as he skulked on the outer reaches of the garden, closer to the walled boundary. "*I thought you were too old to play in the snow,*" she said, communicating with him through her thoughts.

"*Never too old, Birdie, you know that.*" She felt his unbridled joy as he slinked through the snow, his footprints marking the pristine ground.

"*It will take a lot of work to have a fire outside tonight,*" she said thoughtfully. "*The seating pit will take forever to empty out, even with magic. I think we should have a fire on the covered terrace instead.*"

"*Wise,*" he said, making his way to the New Moon Gate in the north. The river of gravel had vanished beneath the snow, but under the gate, where the snow was less deep, Hades paused, sitting on his haunches. "*I can feel the spark of magic here already.*"

Birdie didn't answer that, instead soaking in his experience. She and Hades were bound together, witch and familiar, and had been for most of Birdie's life. She was thirteen when he first found her in the garden, and she had fallen in love with him. He was a beautiful, big cat, with his gorgeous silver and black fur. She hadn't been looking for him, not particularly anyway, but it was probably fair to say that she had been looking for *something*. At thirteen, she was just coming into her powers. Hades had said that he felt her burgeoning magic and had travelled miles to find her. He had never revealed where he had been before, or how old he was, even after all these years, but she had long accepted his need to keep his own past a secret. What did it matter? He was with her now, and would be until she died. He had always promised her that, and unlike her, he hadn't aged a day.

"*Has it changed your plans, Hades, now that I'm younger and hopefully have many years of life left?*"

"*Of course not. I have no plans until you are no longer here. At that point, I will go where I am called.*"

She felt his sincerity, and it comforted her. "*It has unnerved my sons. I'll have to phone Simone to tell her, too. My daughter might be more understanding.*"

"*They are all understanding, Birdie. Just surprised. Wouldn't you be? Especially if Horty were the one gifted with twenty years?*"

Birdie laughed to herself. "*I'd be very annoyed. I must give extra thanks to the Goddess in our celebrations tonight. If Sibilla's gift doesn't change everything.*"

She felt Hades's impatience. "*You must stop worrying and let today's events unfold. You are old enough to know that by now. It's Sibilla. There is nothing to worry about.*"

"*I know. Perhaps I still feel the taint of the Fallen one, Belial, after the other night. His dark presence seems to hover over me, despite our success and the Goddess's intervention. Tonight will banish him for good.*"

As soon as she communicated it, she knew it to be true. Belial's sticky little hands had sullied Moonfell, and she understood what she must do. "*I'll leave you to your hunt, good friend.*"

Returning to her own mind, she found her hands upon the cold sill, her forehead resting on the window. Although she knew where Hades was, she couldn't see him. She smiled, turned, cast a spell to relight the fire that had burned down to embers, and then headed to her private kitchen that was in her suite of rooms. It wasn't as grand as the main kitchen, but it suited her purpose. It still had the huge, Gothic arched windows made of stone, but the room was smaller, and decorated with deep red tiles and units made of cherry wood, very different to Morgana's, which was black and dramatic.

Once done in here, she would find Horty. They could work the spells she had planned together. They didn't need to go back to the library or find anything on Sibilla. Hades was right. It would all unfold as it should. Her job as the head of the coven was to prepare for it, and that's exactly what she would do.

"You two need to become familiar with the glasshouse," Morgana said to Lamorak and Como, "as you both intend to spend more time here, especially if you're moving in."

"You've shown me around here a few times, Mother," Lam said, looking around the immense glasshouse with curiosity. "What more is there to know?"

Como snorted. "Honestly, Lam! You're such a moron. The place is full of poisonous plants..."

"And other plants, too," Morgana reminded them. "Not everything here will kill you or beguile you. There are a lot of herbs and other tender plants here. It's actually a very pleasant place to sit and relax at any time of year. Especially now, more than the summer, really. Look at the snow!" The snow was stacked on the many windowpanes, ice obscuring the light and casting the whole glass house into a milky gloom. "It's wonderful. I must find time to enjoy it later."

The glasshouse was a large half-dome attached to the east wall of the manor house, and could be accessed by a door from the main kitchen, and also a pair of exterior doors that led to the kitchen garden. The dome was made of lots of different shapes of glass all expertly fitted together with iron lattice work. Some pieces were stained glass, and rich ruby and vermillion tones would stretch across the interior in the summer. In the current, muted light they stood out against the snow. This, like the kitchen, was her domain. She knew every plant, nurtured each one, enriched the soil, split the plants and potted them, and generally soaked in the rich, earthy scent. Various seating areas were spread throughout it. A chaise longue covered in throws and cushions lay under one of the windows, a circular table and chairs sat in another area, and a large peacock chair looked to the east and the rising sun. Gravel paths ran between the mix of raised and regular beds, and a long bench was fixed to the house wall, with shelving beneath and stacked with pots, garden tools, and compost. Magic lay across all of it.

As always when she entered this room, she headed to the small altar and lit incense, and then adjusted the temperature. This room was heated all year round, so that no matter how cold it was outside, all the plants would be protected. They thrived in here, just like she did.

"So, Lam," she said, raising an eyebrow at her cheeky son, "show us how good your fantastic memory is by telling me what plants they are." She pointed to the right.

Lam, far taller than her, with his father's grey eyes, shuffled and cleared his throat. "Well, that looks to be digitalis."

"Well done. It was an easy one. And that?" she pointed to another.

"Angelica."

She cocked an eyebrow. "Impressive. And that?" She pointed to a plant with purple berries.

His face wrinkled with confusion, and then his gaze settled on the stack of gardening books on the table. "Er... Hellebore?"

Como snorted. "Belladonna! AKA Deadly Nightshade."

"Since when did you get to be so knowledgeable about plants?" Lam complained.

"Since I decided potions and poisons were cool," he shot back.

Como was shorter than Lam, his dark hair and olive skin tone marking his Italian father's heritage. His big brown eyes were seductive, and Morgana wondered how many women had succumbed to his charm. Lam was fairer, his hair a honey brown, and unlike Como, he wore it long to his collar bone. It had a slight wave to it. He was as good looking and charming as his father, but he hadn't fully grown into it yet. And he was here, choosing her over his father for once, and wanting to hone his magic.

Morgana and he had spoken briefly the night before, when he, a little awkwardly, had admitted he had no idea what he was going to do with his degree when he completed it in the summer, but yes, he would like to discover more of his magic. He and Como had been discussing their plans, that was clear. From the sound of it, they would likely have two young men living in Moonfell over the next year. Morgana was both pleased and trepidatious about it. Maybe they should give them their own suite of rooms, or no one would get any peace.

She brushed it aside for now, aware she had gone quiet while she considered their futures. "Well done, Como. I'm impressed. Is that where you wish to concentrate your magic?"

"And on witch-flight, but I want to learn all of it," he answered, grinning.

"And you, Lam?" Her son hadn't really expanded on that the previous night. "I mean, you're a fire witch, but anything else?"

"Sculpting in metals—using the metals' properties." He blurted it out as if it was a wrench to reveal it. "I've been doing art on the side over the last year. I like the bigness of it."

Morgana smiled. "Using metals' *magical* properties, I presume?"

"I reckon."

"How fantastic. Another artist in the house." Odette painted strange, surreal, and mystical images on canvases that sold very well. The subject matter offered glimpses into other realms with Odette's unique take on it all. The garden looked very different when seen through her eyes. She also painted portraits that were searing in their intensity. Her ability to see to the heart of things sometimes made interesting revelations. "We must find you a big enough space to work, then. The stables, perhaps." She tried to restrain her joy. Lam would be here, creating art and magic.

"I'll need equipment," he said, a gleam of excitement in his eye.

"Not a problem. We'll make a list, and you can inspect the space before you leave."

This is why they needed Moonfell. This is why Sibilla cast the first spell. It gave them space and privacy to practice their magic without outside interference. They had security, too, and it had shielded them from some of the horrors of persecution common in previous centuries.

"However," she continued, "before we get too carried away with our future plans, we must harvest a few last-minute things for our spells tonight. I have already dried some herbs for our protection spell tonight, but we also need fresh herbs and roots." She reeled them off, the list committed to heart after so many years. "After that will be our Yuletide celebration. Another first for both of you as members of this coven."

Como grinned. "I've never been a coven member before."

"Of course you have," Morgana said. "You have always been a member of this coven. The whole family is by birth, until they actively choose otherwise or are cast out."

Lam frowned. "Are many cast out?"

"It isn't unheard of, but it hasn't happened for several decades." She picked up some pairs of gardening gloves and the secateurs. "Lam, please get the basket. Como, follow my instructions. This will be your first introduction into plant preparation for years, I assume, so pay close attention. While we work, we'll run through the plans for tonight again, so you feel fully prepared. Then we'll cook."

Their Yuletide celebrations included eating food around the fire.

"And of course, we need the Yule log. We'll choose one after this."

"Bloody hell," Lam complained, "do we get any rest?"

"Later. Don't worry. It's fun, I promise."

"With the added surprise from Sibilla," Como added.

"That, too." *Whatever it would be.*

The day passed swiftly, but Odette found a few hours in which to paint, leaving her father and her uncle to prepare the covered terrace for the Yule fire. She had no idea where Birdie and Horty had gone. They were being furtive; sneaky, even. That was fine. It seemed there would be a few secrets revealed that evening.

She'd been disappointed not to have another vision through the moon gates the previous night. She had returned to them after the others had gone to bed, but nothing presented itself. They had remained steadfastly ordinary. *Well, as ordinary as they could be.* Of course, the snow still fell thickly, and the temperature had plummeted. She had resigned herself to failure, and went to bed.

However, that morning, and with pressing urgency throughout the day, she had felt the urge to paint, and that urge meant something.

Her studio was on the second floor, in a different wing to the guest bedrooms. It was a remote part of the house, quiet, and more modern. Well, modern was relative. It had been built in the 19th century, so this particular wing had big, square windows, decorative reliefs, and ceiling roses. She had picked this room to be her studio, however, because of its west-facing view, and the sun that spilled in during the afternoon. It was a long room, the ceilings lower because it was on the second floor, and consequently it felt cosier, more intimate.

And it was a mess. Canvases filled every inch of space, stacked against walls and propped on surfaces or easels. Odette sometimes worked on several pieces at once. A long galley kitchen ran off the side, so she had plenty of water and a double sink. She barely saw her surroundings, though.

She found a blank canvas, set up her paints, and started to work the second she set foot in the room. She painted like an automaton, an unseen force directing her hand. She didn't even know what she was painting until it took shape in front of her. Time had no meaning, and dark shadows gathered in the corners of the room while she worked. She flicked a lamp on over her easel by magic and kept going. The house vanished. There was only her and the canvas.

Finally, she stepped back, blinking as she realised that she had painted a room in the original part of the house, but it looked unfamiliar.

It was a small, square space, with arched stone windows, the view outside blurry. She had painted it from the corner, a glimpse of a door to her left, and it had wooden panels on the lower half. The upper part had unusual images painted on the walls. They were rudimentary, naïve artworks, and the furniture was strange.

She had painted a picture of the house from before their time. *But what time was it? Sibilla's?*

Did this room relate to their Yule celebrations, or had something randomly presented itself?

No. It must be about Yule. She tapped her lip, and then realised she'd daubed paint on her face. *Where was this room?* There were so many in Moonfell, and not all were in regular use. She lifted the painting off the easel, and decided to carry it downstairs for reference. She would search the rooms until she found the right one.

Then she realised with a shock as she checked the time on her phone that it was actually time to begin their spells.

Twelve

December 1523

I t was a crisp, cold night when Sibilla led her family outside, their arms loaded with the spell ingredients, and all of them wrapped in cloaks and mufflers.

She had felt at odds all day after visiting her old friends and neighbours in the village. Some had welcomed her, others had looked on with suspicion, but she had stayed for a while regardless, making the rounds, encouraging them to visit her if they needed anything, or send word and she would come. Everyone knew where she lived. Montague Manor was well-known, and had been talked about ever since she was a child. It was understood to be empty, the land becoming overgrown, and now she was living in it.

When she returned to the hall, she had resolved two things. First, that the name must change if it was to become truly theirs, and also that she couldn't change her old neighbours' opinions. Change was a constant, and you either accepted it, or railed against fate and committed yourself to a life of futile regret, and she was too wise to do t hat.

However now, she pushed all of those thoughts aside, and smiled at Mathew. "Are you ready?" He nodded, but she could see the doubt in his eyes. "Do not worry. You will be fine, and your father will help. He has the spell written down, just in case."

"But you will start it with me?" he asked, lip trembling just a little.

"Of course." Her other children were assembled around them, all clutching their own spell ingredients. "We start with our blood. This spell will tie us to the house forever." She caught Rob's eye, and he smiled encouragingly. She took a breath and said, "I brought us here, and unfortunately, it means we've left friends behind. I truly think this move is for the best, although it may also be difficult sometimes. True friends, however, will always stick with us, no matter what. Once we do this spell, we are bound to this house. It will protect us, but I want to reassure you of something." She stared at all her children, one by one. "You are not a prisoner here, understand? It's a home. A refuge, when all else disappoints us. If we choose to travel or live elsewhere in the future, that is all right, but it will always be here for us." She looked back at the house, its windows glowing with candles and witch-lights. "And it will always choose a guardian. I know that to be true. For now it's me, but when one of you is old enough, you will know. But even if you are not chosen, you will always be welcome to live here. Do you offer your blood willingly to bind this house to our family forever?"

It had been a big speech, but her family had listened quietly, and not even Grace had protested. The garden seemed to be listening, too.

"We agree," they all murmured, nodding.

"Good. I have a needle to prick our thumbs, and we'll drop the blood into this herbal mixture. We'll anoint each gate with it, and the central staircase as we work."

Over the next few minutes they worked silently, and when everyone's blood was added to the mixture, Sibilla cast the spell over it. She then blessed the first gate, the New Moon Gate in the north, offering her thanks to the Goddess and Herne the Hunter as she worked. Balance was needed in this, the darkest and longest night of the year.

She snapped her fingers to produce a flame and lit Mathew's candle, and then together they started the first protection spell.

Sibilla felt the magic start to build immediately. The garden was waiting for it, like touching a flame to dry kindling. When Mathew was saying the spell confidently, supported by Rob, she left them to it, and moved to the east gate.

She didn't need to spend long with Rose. She was eager to learn and wanted to continue on her own. This was her gate now and she knew it, and ever since they had cast the first spell, she had visited the east gate every day to tend it like an altar. Rose smeared the bloody herb paste into the yew, uttered her spell, and repeated it with growing confidence. She didn't even register Sibilla leaving.

They moved on again, and Grace didn't even wait for instructions. With a burst of flame and another smear of the bloody herb paste, the spell was cast, and flames bathed the Full Moon Gate, leaving Grace limned in darkness before it.

Sibilla led Beth to the west gate, hoping that Rob would be there to help their youngest, and that Mathew was coping well enough on his own. She should never have doubted him, because when they arrived,

Rob was already waiting. He gave her a brief nod, and she smiled. *Mathew was fine.*

The Waning Moon Gate was the most unusual of the four. It was made of thick ribbons of bronze that wrapped around each other to form the large archway, the metal dull with a heavy patina from age and weathering. A rowan tree grew nearby, its branches leaning over the gate, but otherwise it stood alone in rough grass. It was odd. Unearthly. She would think carefully about how to incorporate it into something larger, but there would definitely be water nearby, and a pond was the best option. Rowan was an interesting choice, too. It was a strong wood, offering protection against magic. For her it represented the Goddess. Rob had planted a wooden torch into the ground, and the flickering flames reflected in the bronze so that it seemed as if the gate was on fire.

She squeezed Beth's hand. "Are you ready?"

Beth looked like a fairy child. Her long, blonde hair tumbled down her back, and her dark eyes looked twice as large in this light. She nodded, eyes fixed on the gate.

"Remember what I said, Beth. When we start this spell, all four gates will link, and then I will go to the house. Your father will stay with you."

Beth held her hand out, not saying a word, already gripped by magic and the spell that was growing over the garden. Sibilla smeared the bloody paste onto her hand, and casting the spell together, Beth rubbed it onto the metal. Magic swelled around them, the protection growing, and she felt it pull from deep within her and then blossom outwards.

Sibilla uttered a word of command, and a shimmering silver light shot up into the sky and then across the garden, each gate connecting to make a giant web. She had placed markers around the perimeter wall earlier that day. Stones, feathers, shells, animal bones, and other natural objects sat at various places, all spelled with protection, and now they connected, too.

It was time for her to go to the house.

"Keep going, Beth," she said, placing her hand on her daughter's head, and nodding to her husband.

Sibilla's skin tingled as she walked through the garden and into the house. The ingredients were waiting by the curving main staircase, and immediately she smeared the herbal paste onto the newel post and up the banister. She continued the spell, feeling the growing magic shoot down into the foundations of the house, and up the staircase and out to the rooms.

She had representations of all four elements with her: a sprig of yew for earth, a feather for air, a chalice of water, and a lit candle for fire. She drew on each of them as she uttered the words that would complete the protection and binding spell. She lit the incense placed ready on a bed of charcoal in a silver dish, repeated her spells, and watched the smoke spread across the house, directed by her words. The scent magnified and the walls of the house seemed to contract and then expand. She placed her hands on the banister again, and silvery light spread up the staircase.

In that moment, she connected mentally to her children and husband, and saw every single moon gate in her mind. She looked through the open front door and saw moonlight flash across the garden in a wave.

Sibilla ran down the steps and onto the drive, looking up with wonder. Over the south gate, easy to see from her position, hovered an image of a full moon. Craning to see to the east and west, she saw magical quarter moons over the waning and waxing gates, and she knew that a dark moon would be hovering in the north.

The images didn't last long, and as they faded, the web that spread across the house faded too, and it seemed that tiny stars fell to the earth like snow. Every part of her felt connected to the house and garden, and her skin shimmered with little pulses of light, like moonbeams.

The name came to her instantly.

Moonfell.

The house would be called Moonfell. For an aspect of the Goddess was the moon, and she would protect them. This would now always be their home.

Sibilla took a deep breath of satisfaction, feeling that their future safety was assured. No matter what anyone might do, the house was theirs. Now that the protection and binding spell was complete, it was time for fun and Yuletide blessings.

And the gift for her descendants.

Thirteen

December 2023

B irdie studied Odette's painting that she'd propped on the sideboard in the formal dining room. "I do not know that room. Are you sure it's in this house?"

"As sure as my insight tells me. Look at the windows! Of course it's here!"

"Perhaps," Morgana suggested cautiously, "it was a small room, but a wall was knocked out and it became larger."

Ellington was behind Birdie, and she could feel him breathing down her neck. "It doesn't look right. The paintings on the wall look odd. Juvenile."

Odette didn't take offence. "I know. They look unfinished, don't they? Like someone was practising art on the walls. Maybe it just didn't translate through my brush."

They had just eaten a light evening meal, something to keep them going until their Yule supper later. There were too many of them to sit comfortably in the main kitchen, so they ate in the splendid surroundings of the dining room, the enormous Christmas tree twinkling with lights and casting a glow across the surfaces. Odette had once again arrived late. She lost track of time when the muse caught her, whether that be while painting or in the garden. Even now, she wasn't quite with them, Birdie noticed. Her mind was elsewhere.

"Did you get any sense of who was behind your...*experience*?" Armstrong asked.

"No. It just happened. I have no idea whether it was male or female, or their age, or the time period, but from the look of the room, I think it would be early on. It has to be about Sibilla. This must be linked to Yule."

"Well, we haven't got time to debate it now," Horty said, her strident tones booming across the room. "We need to start the spell."

They wanted it finished before midnight so they could sit on the terrace and enjoy Yule—and whatever else may happen. Birdie was always aware of the weight of their ancestors, and today she was feeling it more keenly than ever before. Maybe it was her heightened sensibilities after her encounter with the Goddess the other night, or maybe it was five hundred years of Moonfell spells flowing around her.

Birdie nodded, turning her back on the painting to study her assembled family. Her coven, of which she was High Priestess. She was wearing a long, dark red dress, her favourite colour, a dress that had belonged to one of her ancestors. It had embroidery on the sleeves and collar, and she had bound her hair up. It had been a few years since she had been able to dress up for a sabbat. She aimed to celebrate in style. Her family had also dressed up in honour of this particularly special occasion. Morgana was dressed in dark green, another long, heavy dress that had been stored in the attic, and that was Medieval in style. Odette was dressed in black, and Horty was in blue, again both in old fashioned dresses that were kept free of time's ravages by magic and mothballs. Her sons had long robes on over their shirts and trousers, and even Lam and Como wore clothes more suitable for the sixteenth century, donning knee-high boots over their trousers with loose shirts. Everyone would wear cloaks and boots to keep them warm outside. The snow was still falling, although not as thickly as it had been earlier.

"Are the gates clear of snow?" Birdie asked Armstrong.

"They were an hour ago, and I cast a spell on them to keep them that way. The paths are clear, too." He smiled and kissed her cheek. "Can I just say that you look marvellous?"

"Of course you can, any time you like!" She shouldn't have favourites, but Armstong was hers. He was laidback like his father, and didn't feel the need to mansplain or manspread like his younger brother. Nevertheless, she gave Ellington a beaming smile, too. It wasn't often they visited at the same time. "Let us begin."

Morgana had cast these protection spells for years. She was so familiar with them that it was like slipping into old clothes.

Tonight, however, felt different, especially with Lamorak here. They were together at the Full Moon Gate, snow swirling gently around them, the cold nibbling at their skin.

"So, you're normally on the north gate?" Lam asked her, fidgeting as he readied himself for the spell. "The New Moon Gate?"

"Yes, I'm an earth witch, so that's where I'm strongest, but you're here, and you need help. Plus, Birdie wanted to mix things up."

"But that's okay, right?"

"Of course. Don't worry. You're not at risk, and this is merely a protection spell. Just because I'm at a different gate makes no odds to me. The words are the same, but the ingredients are different." She hesitated, not wanting him to be uncomfortable, but then threw caution to the wind. "I'm glad you're here. This is a good age to embrace your magic. At an important sabbat, too. Thank you for coming."

"I've felt the pull of it more and more lately. I can't ignore it. Dad says I shouldn't, either. He said it's important."

"Did he?" Morgana was stunned. It was her magic that had driven them apart. "Well, that's shockingly generous."

He was tight-lipped, wary of criticism towards his father. "He can be."

Morgana recognised that tone and moved on. "I'm glad. We're all happy to see you here, and very happy that you might move in." She stopped as she felt the creep of magic across her skin. Power was building already. The house knew it was time. "Can you feel it?"

"Feel what?"

"Close your eyes, and let your senses explore. The house is releasing some of its magic. It always does on this night. It's like it's ready to be renewed, and knows what's coming. It feels like a tickle on your skin, a feather-kiss on your cheek."

Excitement flushed Lam's face while he did as she asked. "A tingle. Like pins and needles."

He looked so innocent for a moment, with his eyes closed and face raised, so like a child again, and a rush of love flooded through her. "Exactly." She checked her watch. Unlike when Sibilla had cast the first spell, they would all begin together at ten-thirty promptly. Not that she needed her watch. Birdie would announce the time for everyone. Right on cue, a huge bell resounded across the grounds; a deep toll that shuddered through her. "That's it. Time to begin."

As they'd discussed, they rubbed the bloody herbal mixture into the gate, uttering the first words of the spell as they did so. Immediately, witch-fire flashed across the gate, swiftly followed by a soft white light, and silvery threads shot into the air. She could see the east and west gate from their position, and light from their magic filtered into the night sky above them. Against the backdrop of the snow, it was ethereal. The family's blood added an extra potency this year, and as her hair rose on her skin, it confirmed that something was different this year. *Very* different.

Snow was caught up in the wind that wound around Odette and Como in the east.

Odette nodded encouragingly, noting Como's startled expression.

They repeated the words together, their magic combining with the strands that emanated from the other gates. Every year it was layered afresh, old building on new, unaffected by the weather. Odette had the feeling that even if something catastrophic were to happen, and the spell wasn't cast for years, there was enough power already around the house to sustain it for some time. *Not that they would ever risk it, though.*

Como gasped as white light flashed through him, lifting his hair like static electricity, and his eyebrows rose with shock. Odette couldn't help giggling. This was magic. This was *power*. And Moonfell was full of it.

Then she gasped, too. An image was forming in the gate, and another figure became clear to her. A young girl, confidently casting the spell on her own, her face uplifted to the sky. A name flashed into her mind. *Rose*. Sibilla's daughter.

However, Rose was unaware of Odette. She was a vision only. A link to the first spell because of the strength of their present one. The past was reaching out on this auspicious night. It felt like a blessing from Sibilla herself.

Another flash of light distracted Odette and she looked to the north, where her father was, and laughed with joy. All the gates were lit up now. She could see the glow of the west gate from her position, cresting over the roof of the house. It illuminated the spinning weathervane by the chimneys. The spell was close to complete now.

A huge beam of white light shot from the top of the biggest chimney. It pierced the sky before it scattered across the garden and connected to the web created by the moon gates. Another flash of light followed, rippling across the web, and Odette felt as if she was being hugged. The house was happy, the spell was complete, and the vision of Rose vanished.

She fell silent, and Como followed suit. "Can you feel it, Como?"

He nodded, dazed. "Holy shit, Odette. That was...immense."

"I know. It's a big spell, and incredible that Sibilla cast it with her children. It's a mark of her power, or maybe just her determination. But did you *feel* it?"

"The squeeze? It was how it feels like when I see Horty for the first time in months. She nearly crushes me."

Odette nodded with satisfaction. "Good. The house has welcomed you into its fold. All is well."

"So Birdie is done inside?"

"She should be. Let's go and see."

But Como hung back. "Why did Sibilla cast such a big spell after being in the house for just weeks? You would have thought she would have lots to do first."

Odette shrugged. "I think it was just the natural thing to do. She started the new grimoire at the same time. I assume it was all about new beginnings. Not that it says much in the grimoire about it."

"No, I noticed that yesterday with Morgana. There are just annotations to spells. I have my own book, you know, but it's a bit scrappy. It's made me realise I should pay more attention to my own."

"Another excellent outcome to tonight, then!"

And then something totally unexpected happened. The protection spell had been fading, the darkness settling around them like a cloak once more, but now, bright white lights like a shower of fireworks shot out of the chimneys and scattered across the garden.

"What the hell is that?" Como said, transfixed on the sight.

"I think that is what Birdie and Horty have been up to all day."

The white lights danced, zigzagged, and fizzed, and stars formed out of them, falling like confetti to the ground.

Odette smiled. "It's an after-show."

"It doesn't normally happen?"

"No. But you'd think they'd be outside to see it." Odette stood for a few moments more, admiring the falling stars conjured by magic.

"It's brilliant." Como was smiling, hands flexing, and she knew he wanted to join in.

"Go on! Like this." Odette cast the spell to conjure her own stars and blew them into the garden. "Use air to scatter them, Como."

Como let loose, and soon sparkling white stars were drifting across the gardens like the sky had fallen.

She realised then that she'd missed Birdie. Over long months she had acclimatised to her age and failing health, but there had been a gap. A hole in their eccentric day to day lives in Moonfell. Now Birdie was back, she was as naughty as ever.

"Don't ever think life gets boring as you get older," Odette said to Como. "Not if you do it right, anyway."

"What do you mean?"

"I mean that there comes a point when you cease to give a crap about anybody else's opinions. I'm not quite there yet, but Morgana is, and so is Birdie. How very liberating. Let's enjoy this a little longer before we go in."

Birdie was giggling with her sister in the hall, both of them like children as they finished the protection spell on the central staircase.

Horty pointed out the open door. "Look what we did! It's quite impressive, if I do say so myself."

"Did you ever doubt us?"

"Not really." Horty cast her eyes to the floor and then back to Birdie again, suddenly serious. "I shouldn't have been cross yesterday...about your age, I mean. It's lovely to see you looking so good and full of energy again. I've missed this."

"Not as much as I have!" She hugged her sister. "Thank you. I hope you keep your health better than I did, and then we can do more of this."

"I'll certainly try." Horty looked out the front door again as their spell continued to zip around the garden. "Look at Morgana and Lam. Isn't it nice to see them together?"

"It's about time." Birdie was about to say something detrimental about her ex-son-in-law, but stopped herself. *Not tonight.* "It's good that Como wants to move in, too. I told you years ago that Jemima wouldn't have it all her own way. The house finds a way with those it wants."

Horty swelled with pleasure. "I'm so pleased that he'll be closer. I think Anton will be much more encouraging with his children." Horty had two children, of which Anton was the youngest, at 52. He had two children who were 12 and 10. Anton didn't visit Moonfell much either, but he was far less antagonistic about it. "I'll have to visit here more often, and maybe bring them along."

A *clunk* from under the staircase stopped their conversation.

"Did you hear that?" Horty asked, hands raised, magic balling in her palms as she cautiously edged under the sweeping staircase.

It was enormous, made of polished wood, the newel posts carved to look like stag heads, which had effectively stopped the children from trying to slide down them as young troublemakers. They would have been impaled. *A clever deterrent.* Not that she had considered it so as a child herself.

It was dark beneath the stairs, lit only by the Christmas tree lights. Natural light rarely penetrated there even in the day, but they had a table beneath it, and on it was lamp and a basket where they deposited mail and other detritus. It was also where Odette liked to lurk and surprise unwitting visitors.

"Has something fallen off the table?" Birdie asked, eyes automatically checking the floor.

"Oh no, my dear. Look!" Horty pointed above their head, and a few feet above them, set into a tread under the stairs, a large drawer had popped open.

"Sibilla's surprise," Birdie said, almost breathless with excitement. "Odette was right! Go summon the others! Quickly!"

While Horty magically made the deep bell toll over the house and grounds, Birdie wondered how best to retrieve the drawer. Magic would work, but she didn't want to risk whatever was inside. *Ladders, perhaps?*

Within minutes, everyone had assembled, stamping snow off their boots, faces flushed with the excitement of the spell and the cold. A nimbus of power clung to all of them.

"Love your spell, Birdie," Como said enthusiastically. "Brilliant. In fact, the whole thing was brilliant."

Birdie waved his compliment off. "Something else has happened. Look!"

"Super cool," Lam said, nodding. "A hidden compartment."

"Why on Earth is it so high?" Ellington complained.

"If there are joins in the wood, no one would see them up there. Maybe she was worried the magic that contained it would fail after all these years," Morgana suggested.

"Who cares?" Birdie asked, impatience eating her up. "How do we get to it?"

"Come on, Odette," Lam said, crouching. "You look the lightest. Get on my shoulders. It will be quicker than a ladder."

"Dear boy," Ellington said, "magic is quicker than all of that."

"Don't you dare break it," Birdie warned him, knowing it was impossible to stop him.

"Mother, please."

Ellington always had a gift with making objects move, and he wiggled his fingers, uttered a spell, and the drawer shot out and landed in his hands with such force that he let out his breath with a *woosh*, staggered back, and had to be supported by an amused Lamorak.

"Nice one, Uncle Ellington."

Birdie bustled over. "You better not have damaged it. Put it on the table."

Something was in the drawer, wrapped in linen and straw, and Birdie carefully lifted it out, unwrapping the layers slowly.

"It's a model of the house!" She held it close to the lamp, and they all crowded around.

The house was set on a base, with four moon gates included around it to mimic the garden. It was beautiful in its detail, and the wood felt warm to her skin. She turned it around, noting the windows and courtyard, and steps to the front door.

"It's smaller than it is now," Como observed.

"It's the original house, before all the additions," Morgana told him. "The west wing was built in the eighteenth century, and the conservatory in the nineteenth. And of course, there have been lots of interior renovations. The family thrived here, and their magic was in demand—discreetly, of course, and with people who had money."

"The stables were original, though, even though they're not part of this design," Armstrong said, "but they were extended, too." He put on his reading glasses and lifted it from his mother's hands. "Whoever carved it put the courtyard in, as well. Look at the detail. It must have been done in sections, but there's no sign of a join."

Lam shrugged. "Could it have been carved with magic?"

"It's possible, but I doubt it," Armstrong said. "Whoever did this had skills we don't know about."

"Sibilla," Odette corrected her father, "not just anyone."

"We don't know that for sure."

He was right, Birdie mused. She herself had many magical abilities, but she couldn't carve wood with such accurate detail, and she doubted Odette could, either, although she could paint very well.

"You left something in the drawer," Odette said, lifting out a sheet of paper that had been hidden under the package. "It's signed by Sibilla! We were right!" She flashed her father a look of triumph.

"*You* were right," Horty corrected her. "Get on with it. What does it say?"

Odette's lips twisted with mischief as she scanned the page. "The language is tricky, but essentially it's a question about a spell. She asks which moon gate was the first one to be tied to the moon's phases?"

"The first one. The north moon gate," Ellington said confidently.

"Idiot. The east gate—air," Birdie said, casting him a withering glance. "It was a waxing moon, and she started with that gate. The north was cast out of phase, and she had to repeat it after the Yule spell."

"How do you know that?" Lam asked.

"It's in the spell book," Como answered. "I saw it yesterday. Very cool!"

Horty shushed him. "What now, Odette?"

She pushed her hair from her face, eyes fixed on the paper. "We're running out of time. We need to be at that gate at midnight! It's a rhyme, and it says, '*The witching hour is full of power and spells that have lain dormant, but choose the gate, and cast the spell, and the house will lead you forward.*' Does this mean *that* house?" She nodded at the carved house that appeared so innocuous.

"It must do, or why leave the message with it?" Armstong said. He had taken his cloak off in the house, but pulled it around his shoulders again with a flourish. "How long have we got?"

"It's eleven-thirty," Morgana said, checking the time on the huge clock decorated with arcane symbols in the hall. "Half an hour."

"I'm hoping you have mulled wine on the hob, Morgana?" he asked.

"Yes, why?"

"Good." He winked. "Let's grab a glass while someone fetches Sibilla's grimoire, and take it all with us. Who knows where this little game may lead us."

Fourteen

December 2023

With a glass of mulled wine heating her hands, Morgana felt fortified for whatever lay ahead, and she silently cast a warming spell to warm her feet as well.

The whole family was assembled by the Waxing Moon Gate, and once again snow was gently falling like tiny feathers, dusting the cleared ground. There was an air of anticipation...or maybe she was just imagining it. Lam and Como were talking in hushed whispers, and she restrained a smile. The two young men may have been around magic all their lives, but she knew the wonder of it had escaped them. Lam's father had bred distrust and suspicion, and Como's mother had been put out about the house, and no matter what Horty had said, Como hadn't really taken it in. However, they were adults now and could make their own minds up about it, and tonight was definitely swaying them in the right direction. Well, a direction that a witch approved of, at least. It also helped that Uncle Ellington and her father were there; two powerful male witches who wielded their magic with a flourish. Role models. Although, Morgana liked to think that the three residents of Moonfell were better role models. *Time would tell.*

Birdie had carried the carved wooden house on its tiny garden almost reverently, and now she placed it on the ground in a patch cleared of snow. Lam had carried the ancient family grimoire. It was huge and heavy, but he handled it with ease.

"Right, well. Let's hope this works." Birdie swept her scarf around her neck and smoothed her hair away from her face. "Hold the book open for me, Lam. Yes, that page, please." Taking a deep breath, she uttered the spell that had originally bound the gate to the waxing moon, repeating it several times for effect.

Nothing happened.

"What have we done wrong?" Como asked.

Morgana checked the time. "It's virtually midnight. Maybe you should say it again?"

"Maybe," Horty suggested, "the moon's phase needs to be right, too."

Ellington snorted. "Well, unless Sibilla was a first-rate astronomer, she could have hardly known what phase the moon would be in now."

"Shush!" Odette said sharply. "I saw Rose here earlier, while we were casting the spell. This was hers. She was an air witch. Como should try."

"How do you know?" Lam asked.

"It's what I do."

"But what if we didn't have one?" Birdie asked, floundering.

"I don't know, but can we please try? Time is running out!" Morgana said. *If they missed their opportunity, would that be it forever?*

"But I don't know this spell," Como said, anguished.

"Neither did I!" Birdie pointed out. "Read it out! *With intention!*"

The witch-light bobbed over the page, and Como scanned the writing. He started the spell hesitantly.

All eyes were on the wooden house on the ground, a wariness to everyone, as they had no idea what might happen. Morgana, however, caught Como's eye and mouthed, *Again*.

Becoming familiar with the old-fashioned language, he repeated it several times with growing conviction, but still, nothing happened. It was now past midnight, but perhaps the witching hour could be counted as the hour from midnight until one.

Ellington huffed, scooped the house off the ground, and thrust it at Como. "Hold it."

"What if it explodes?"

"Sibilla is hardly likely to have given a gift to her ancestors that she secured the house for only to kill us, you idiot. Again."

The tension was now palpable, and everyone held their breath as Como repeated the spell. This time, however, more aware of passing time, he said it with conviction. Command, even.

"That's more like it," Horty muttered.

No one responded because everyone was staring at the wooden replica of the house. Something was happening. A swirl of white light had manifested around it, and then seemingly *in* it. Everyone leaned closer as Como raised his hands so they could see it easily. It was as if every single little window lit up.

And then, one by one, every light blinked out.

Birdie's hands flew to her cheeks. "They've gone!"

"Not on this side," Armstrong said, almost bouncing with glee. Morgana hadn't seen her father so excited in years. "A little light is burning in the second-floor window, facing south." He turned and pointed. "Third window in from the left."

For a second, Odette was caught unawares. It was as if her uncle had lit a stick of dynamite in front of them, and Birdie was the first to respond.

"One of the bedrooms. Let's go!" Birdie said, racing off with impressive speed, cloak flapping behind her.

Everyone leaped into action and ran after her, but Odette bolted through the others, hot on her grandmother's heels. Lamorak would probably have been one of the quickest had he not been carrying the huge grimoire, but he still overtook Armstrong and Ellington.

Odette ran past Birdie, who shouted, "Oh no, you don't!" She flicked a spell at her feet, but Como had overtaken Birdie now too, and it missed Odette and hit Como instead. He tumbled to the ground, landing in the snow in a tangle of limbs, and tripped Morgana up, too.

Odette giggled, scooped up a snowball, and flung it behind her, hitting Birdie in the chest.

The race to the house descended into mayhem. Spells and snowballs were zinging back and forth, but Odette kept her lead. She raced through the house, trying to beat everyone else to the room, very relieved that Como hadn't mastered witch-flight yet. Unfortunately, the stairs and her long dress were slowing her down, and her father was catching up—until Como smacked him in the back with a spell and he dropped to his knees.

"Como!" he bellowed. "You bastard!"

Como literally trod on him to pass him, and Ellington couldn't fire off a spell quick enough.

Consequently, everyone was held up by Ellington's ungainly floundering, and Odette and Como made the final sprint alone. Odette tried to remember how many windows were in each room as she ran along the second-floor hallway. *Which room was the right one?*

"Bloody hell, you're quick!" Como complained behind her, sounding horribly close.

She glanced at him, just in time to see him aim a bolt of power at her back. She threw a protection spell behind her, and his magic rebounded, hit him in the chest, and he crashed to the floor instead.

"Cheat!" Como roared.

"You started it!"

Odette magically threw each door open, before finally skidding through the door that led into the second to last room. She flicked the lights on, and stopped dead just beyond the doorway. Como, who had regained his feet quickly, smacked into her, almost sending her sprawling.

"What the hell are you stopping for, Odette?" Then he gasped. "Oh! Wow!"

The room was another guest bedroom that wasn't currently in use as it was normally taken by Aunt Simone when she visited. On three walls it was decorated in elegant, sea green chinoiserie wallpaper, with delicate branches filled with camelias and birds, including the wall in which two large, Gothic windows were situated. However, the fourth wall, behind the bed, was panelled in wood, and one of the large panels was ajar, revealing a dark interior.

"A secret panel," Odette said, catching her breath after the furious sprint. "I'm nervous to look!"

"I'm not," Como said, stepping around her.

Her hand shot out and gripped his elbow. "We need to wait for the others. It wouldn't be right to see it first."

"Then why did I half-kill myself racing to get up here?"

She laughed. "For the fun of it!"

Within a few moments, the others arrived, and Birdie squeezed her shoulder. "Thank you for waiting."

Horty was the last to join them, wheezing with the exertion. "If I didn't know better, I'd say you were all trying to kill me. Oh! That's new. I thought I knew all the secret passages and cupboards in this house."

"Secret passages?" Como said, eyebrow cocked. "Cool!"

Lam placed the grimoire on Simone's bed. "Well, who's going to look first? Come on!"

"We all are," Birdie crossed the room, the others behind her, and she opened the door carefully. The hinges were stiff and groaned as she pulled the door wide open. Inside, looking as pristine as the day it was made thanks to magic, was a much bigger wooden model of Moonfell. There wasn't a garden around it this time, though. It was just the house, but it was as tall as Birdie, and a true work of art.

"Oh my Goddess," Birdie said, hands clasped in front of her. "It's enormous. Does it open?"

"Come on, Lam," Como said, squeezing into the hidden cupboard. "Let's move it into the room so we can find out."

After several minutes of gentle manoeuvring, in which everyone joined in as the access became easier, the house stood in the centre of the Persian rug.

"It's absolutely perfect," Odette said, taking it all in.

There were the two original towers, the sloping roofs, the many chimneys, the great Gothic windows, and all the embellishments on the stonework, even down to the Green Man and the grotesque gargoyles on some of the spouting. The courtyard was also beautifully designed.

Lam leaned forward, eyes narrowing. "I spy a latch. Shall I?" Everyone nodded, and he gently swung the entire front of the house open. However, it wasn't the front wall of the house that opened; instead, the house split in two, hinging open so that two sides swung back, revealed the interior of the courtyard and its walls.

"There's another latch on this side," Como said, bending down to release it.

Armstrong nodded. "And one here."

Little by little, they opened up panels to reveal the furnished interior of the house. Odette was feeling emotional, and was relieved to see she wasn't the only one. Morgana was blinking back tears, and Horty was on her knees, peering inside like a child.

Horty squealed with joy. "It's a Moonfell doll's house. Look! It's decorated for Yule in the hall. Look at the staircase." She pointed to where sprigs of greenery were wrapped around the banister.

Ellington whistled. "This is magnificent. It must have taken months, if not years to make by a craftsman. It's probably worth a fortune! Not that we'd ever sell it, obviously," he added hurriedly after Armstrong glared at him.

Odette knew that the doll's house, much like the real one, would no doubt contain secrets. Messages from Sibilla and her children, perhaps. She crouched to examine the rooms, and then spotted a familiar one. "I drew this room! No wonder the wall art looked odd. It's a child's drawing!"

Morgana crouched next to her. "You had a vision of this room, not a real one. That's...astonishing."

A tingle ran through Odette. "I must have linked with the making of this, the decoration of it. I feel emotional!"

Morgana smiled. "Me, too. What a gift!"

Birdie, however, was transfixed on the tower, the one with the room they used for spellcasting, and she eased the side of it open. A miniature spell room lay inside, lined with shelves and bottles. *Sibilla's spell room, no doubt.*

Even more intriguing, in the middle of the room, was a rolled-up sheet of parchment—full-sized, a red ribbon around it, and a seal on the paper.

"Go on, Birdie," Odette said, nudging her gently. "It must be from Sibilla. One High Priestess to another."

With trembling fingers and a nervous smile, Birdie picked it up. "Let's take everything downstairs and read the letter by the fire. I need food and a drink for this."

Fifteen

November 1524 and December 2023

S ibilla looked at the incredible house that her husband and Mathew had made together, and then at the pair of them, silently
watching her.

"It's magnificent," she said, "I can't believe it."

Rob nudged his son. "It would be good if your mother had a little more faith in us."

"That's not what I mean!"

He winked and kissed her cheek. "I know. Is this what you wanted?"

"It's better than I ever dreamed of. It's…" She faltered, trying to find the right words. "It's a precious gift."

"One too good to put into storage right now," he said. He looked at their son with pride. "Mathew used magic on it, too, while he was carving."

Mathew nodded. "Little spells for luck and protection, like charms. There are little sprigs of lavender in there, too. I picked them in the summer."

She hugged him, ruffling his hair. "You're very clever, and I'm very proud of you. Your magic has come on this year."

Almost a full year had passed since their first Yule in the house, and the cold, dark days of winter had descended again. That's how long it had taken Rob and Matt to make the house, around their other projects. They had worked together in the stables, as well as in the house at night. It was a labour of love. She had only seen sections of it before, and knew it would be big, but this was something else.

Full of pride, Matt added, "I helped carve the furniture, too."

"Open it up and show your mother," Rob instructed.

Over the next few minutes they showed her the house, the decorations, the secret cupboards and doors, and Sibilla realised that Rob was right. There was no way she could just put this away in a cupboard, sealed with a spell for five hundred years. This achievement demanded to be played with and used. All the children would love it. They could accumulate other little gifts to put in it, hidden in secret corners. It would be like a treasure trove.

She looked at Rob. "You're right. We'll keep it around for a few years, really finish it, fill it with magic, then I'll seal it up with a letter inside. A message for our descendants."

"You're very sure this place will still be with them, aren't you."

"The spell was strong. We'll repeat it again this year, and then every year into the future. I'll tell whoever reads it why I did it." She glanced at Mathew, aware he was listening. "Matt, run and fetch your sisters, and you can show them everything, too."

"You don't need to fear Catherine," Rob said, once Mathew had left. "She's pregnant again, thanks to you."

"I know, but still, it's good to be sure. People do unexpected things sometimes, and look what we've done to this house already. What if she decides she wants it back for her children?"

In the past year, they had made Moonfell a home, filling it with love and magic. She had planned out the gardens, years of future work, but the kitchen garden and her herbs were already well underway. Despite her issues of the year before, some of her old neighbours still wanted her help, and she had new customers now, too. Wealthy ones. In addition, Robert's business was doing well, and he spent hours in the stables that had been converted into a workshop.

There was already too much invested of them in the house, so yes, she would continue its spells and explain why in her letter. She had kept the details to a minimum in the family grimoire, and her descendants would know little to nothing about Rob. It was something she aimed to rectify. He was as much a part of the house as the witches. He'd added his own magic here.

"You'll still tie it to the Yuletide spell though, from last year?"

"Yes. It will need a few magical adjustments, but it will work fine. Eventually, though. Not just yet. I think that when Beth is a few years older, sixteen perhaps, I'll hide the house then, in a place even the children don't know about."

"Sneaky wife," he said kissing her.

"I know." She laughed, looking forward to her and her family's future, and hoping that her plans would work.

The covered terrace at the west of the house is perfect for winter, Birdie thought, as she settled in a cushioned chair, blankets spread over her legs.

It was sheltered from wind and rain—and now snow—courtesy of the wide, pitched roof that had been erected over the irregularly shaped area wedged between where one part of the house met another. The winter terrace, as it was simplistically called. It was a later addition, early twentieth century, and they had furnished it with comfortable chairs, low tables, subtle lighting, and an outside sofa, as well as a large brazier for a fire.

Fallen leaves sometimes made their way in here, but her sons had swept it out earlier, and now with fairy lights and candles placed in nooks and crannies and lanterns, it was perfect for their Yuletide gathering.

She'd snacked on some cheese and crackers, but that was all she'd had the patience to eat; she wanted to read Sibilla's letter. Making sure her hands were clean, she cracked the seal and unrolled the letter, revealing several sheets wrapped within.

"Ready?" she said to everyone.

They all nodded, hands filled with food and drink.

"As you can imagine, the language is archaic, so I'll modernise as I go. Bear with me."

Dear descendant, whoever you are, I hope this letter finds you well.

I trust that if you're reading this, that you are a witch and have found this house, our gift from the first Moonfell family, to you.

Of course, it is possible that something terrible befell the family that I and all of my spells and plans could not foresee, and that our protection has failed somehow, through lack of renewal, perhaps, and that someone has smashed the panelling and found this house intended for you. In which case, you are an interloper. I hope you treat this house—both of them, actually—kindly.

But I choose to believe that we Moonfell witches are far too wise to let that happen, and that we cherish the house that has kept us safe for centuries. Well, for you at least.

For me and my family, it has been now eight years since Baroness Catherine Montague and her husband gifted old Montague Manor to us. I have written a few words about this in the front of our grimoire, so trust you know how the house came to be ours—if the grimoire has survived through time. It was a present for bringing Catherine's baby to term after many failed pregnancies. He is a son and an heir for a desperate husband and wife.

However, within weeks of moving here, I sensed that perhaps Catherine, as she encouraged me to call her, might change her mind, or use the house as some kind of blackmail. Or even demand it back, should the whim take her. I choose to trust very few people. It has kept me in good stead.

The house was crying out for attention when we moved in. It was solid in build, but neglected in heart, and the garden had run wild. The moon gates lay in tangles of grass and plants, but I saw its potential, even then. It welcomed us, and from the day I set foot in it, I knew it was destiny. It seems the bees did, too. The original bee hives had been here long before the house. I hope their descendants are there still, and trust that you follow bee lore. The bees told Beth that we must tie the protection spell to the moon gates. They considered them special. I have never found out why.

Consequently, I decided to take no risks, and deter-mined to cast a spell on the house and grounds to secure it for our future. Catherine's behaviour within weeks of us moving in reinforced my determination. I decided on a new grimoire for the new house, and as you know, dear witch, cast the first spells on the moon gates, tying them to the phases of the moon. I have embellished these over the last few years, and will no doubt do more in years to come. However, the protection and binding spell was of more import.

I trust that the family is still reinforcing them.

Now, to return to the model of the house. It was my daughter Beth's suggestion to make a gift for you with-in days of us moving in. She is uncanny, even when younger. I debated several ideas before a model house presented itself. It seemed perfect. My husband, Rob, a good and honest man, is a carpenter, and highly skilled. Mathew, our son and a witch, is his apprentice.

They made it together, and it took almost a full year. We decided not to hide it away as soon as it was made, as I originally intended, so the house has been a play-

thing for our children. They have been gentle with it, but there were knocks and scratches over the years. You will find them if you search hard enough. I could have spelled them away, but I think having something that has been used with much love is better than something too clean and perfect.

I won't give away any of its secrets; instead, I hope you smile and laugh as you discover them at your leisure. The children—although I can hardly call Grace and Rose that now, as they are truly young women—have taken great pleasure in hiding gifts in it...magic too, of course.

As for Catherine, I was right. She has four very healthy children now, but she covets this house, even though she also tells me how much it suits me. No demands have been made as yet, but I sense she may try to own it again one day.

She will fail.

I believe that the Goddess chose to bless me—us—with this house, so I will continue to work as much good as

my magic and skills allow over the coming years to show
my gratitude. I hope she continues to rain her blessings
down upon us.

Enjoy your Yule celebrations, dear descendant, and may
Moonfell continue to sustain us for another five hun-
dred years.

Yours with much love,

Sibilla Selcouth

Birdie looked through the window into the adjoining room, a winter sitting room, where the Moonfell model house sat in full view on
a table. "So, her husband and son made the model. How wonderful."
She felt a little shaky, and took a few deep breaths to steady herself.

Armstrong nodded. "A whole year! Doesn't surprise me. They
must have carved the furniture, too."

"And there are other little gifts in it," Horty said, twisting in her seat
to look at the model house. "I'm going to explore all of it tomorrow.
Every single room. I bet the fabrics once graced these rooms."

"And the paint," Odette agreed.

Como prodded the fire with a big stick. "Do we still have bees?"

"Absolutely," Birdie said, thinking that she must tell the bees about
their latest activities. "They are still in the orchard, and they gift us

fabulous honey every year. We must introduce you to them, even though they're sleeping. It's rude not to. It doesn't surprise me that they were here back then, although I didn't actually realise that." Although, perhaps it was in Sibilla's diaries that she'd never read. *Something to amend.*

Odette was curled up in a large outdoor chair, a rug over her knees as she sipped wine. She stared into the fire, her gaze absent. "How terrible the sneaky Catherine was, though. Poor Sibilla must have been so worried she would somehow try to get it back."

"She might not have," Horty said with a sigh. "Four healthy children could have become sick at any point, especially back then. She would have wanted to keep Sibilla on her side, I'm sure."

"Canny, though," Ellington said. He had his feet propped up on the brick edge that surrounded the fire-filled brazier, warming them, his hands cupping a glass of whiskey. "Very wise to take such precautions."

Armstrong nodded, face hidden half in shadow. "She was clearly a very gifted witch, and very determined. A trait that has been passed down through generations. We're a strong-willed bunch."

"But clearly," Morgana mused, "she was the start of our family's connection to nobility, in past generations. To have such powerful friends would have been helpful."

"Not if you wronged them, though," Como pointed out. "I must start looking into our history more. I don't feel I've appreciated it enough."

"That's okay," Birdie reassured him. "We get on with our day to day lives. We can't always be looking over our shoulder to the past. We have to look forward, too. And I very much am. Are you both moving in then, in the summer?" she asked Como and Lamorak.

"I am," Como agreed. "What about you, Lam?"

He nodded, glancing at his mother first. "Yes, if that's okay?"

"Of course it is," Birdie said. "You are always welcome. Make sure to pick your rooms."

Morgana's lips twitched with amusement. "I was thinking, perhaps some shared rooms for them? You know, a sitting area and other common spaces, so they aren't stuck socialising with us when they don't want to." Birdie tried not to laugh, knowing exactly what Morgana meant. *And so that we don't have to put up with them.*

"Excellent thinking. We shall investigate that tomorrow."

It struck Birdie that Sibilla was right. The Goddess has been generous to them. Particularly, the other night. She had gifted her more years, and now she could enjoy the change coming to the house, because every few years something shook them up, and she had a feeling they were entering one of those fresh phases. Change was coming, and change was good—mostly.

What a night. And what a Yule.

Birdie raised her glass. "A toast everyone! To Yule, past and present. Bottoms up!"

Thanks for reading *The First Yule.* Please make an author happy and leave a review. There will be another book in this series coming soon.

The next book to be released will be Storm Moon Shifters Book Two.

Newsletter

If you enjoyed this book and would like to read more of my stories, please <u>subscribe to my newsletter</u> at tjgreenauthor.com. You will get two free short stories, *Excalibur Rises* and *Jack's Encounter,* and will also receive free character sheets for all of the main White Haven witches.

By staying on my mailing list you'll receive free excerpts of my new books, as well as short stories, news of giveaways, and a chance to join my launch team. I'll also be sharing information about other books in this genre you might enjoy.

Ream

I have a started my own subscription service called Happenstance Book Club. I know what you're thinking! What is Ream? It's a bit like Patreon, which you may be more familiar with, and it allows you to support me and read my books before anyone else.

There is a monthly fee for this, and a few different tiers, so you can choose what tier suits you. All tiers come with plenty of other bonuses, including merch for the top two tiers, but the one thing common to all is that you can read my latest books while I'm writing them – so they're a rough draft. I will post a few chapters each week, and you can read them at your leisure, as well as comment in them. You can also choose to be a follower for free.

You can comment on my books, chat about spoilers, and be part of a community. I will also post polls, character art, and some of my earlier books are available to read for free.

Interested? Head to Happenstance Book Club.

https://reamstories.com/happenstancebookclub

Happenstance Book Shop

I also now have a fabulous online shop called Happenstance Books where you can buy eBooks audiobooks, and paperbacks, many bundled up at great prices, as well as fabulous merchandise. I know that you'll love it! Check it out here: https://happenstancebookshop.com/

Read on for a list of my other books.

Author's Note

T hank you for reading *The First Yule,* the first book about the
Moonfell witches.

From the moment I started writing about them in Storm Moon
Rising, Storm Moon Shifters Book 1, I knew I had to write more about
them. Then they popped up in Immortal Dusk, and I was smitten.
From the response of all of my readers, I knew you were eager to read
more about them too. I hope that you have enjoyed this book.

There will be a full-length book in this series next year, and at this
stage I aim to keep it a mix between present and past, with lots of great
characters, mysteries, and paranormal shenanigans. And that fabulous
house!

If you'd like to read a bit more background on the stories, please
head to my website www.tjgreenauthor.com, where I blog about the
books I've read and the research I've done for the series. In fact, there's
lots of stuff on there about my other two series, Rise of the King and
White Haven Hunters, as well.

I also now have an online shop called Happenstance Books, where
you can buy all of my eBooks, paperbacks, audiobooks, hardbacks, and
merchandise. www.happenstancebookshop.com.

In addition, I now offer a subscription community called Happenstance Book Club. I offer early access to work in progress chapters and

so much more. Check it out here: https://reamstories.com/happens
tancebookclub

Talking of Ream, I owe a big thanks to Gilly Taito, one of my sub-
scribers, who suggested Sibilla's surname, Selcouth. It is Middle-Eng-
lish via Old English and means "strange, unusual, rare, unfamiliar,
marvellous, and wondrous." How perfect!

I'd also like to let you know that all of my audiobooks are on my
YouTube channel, so please subscribe, and you can listen to them for
free! https://www.youtube.com/@tjgreenauthor

Thanks again to Fiona Jayde Media for my awesome cover, and
thanks to Kyla Stein at Missed Period Editing for applying your fabulous editing skills.

Thanks also to my beta readers—Terri and my mother. I'm glad
you enjoyed it; your feedback, as always, is very helpful! Thanks also
to Jase, my fabulously helpful other half. You do so much to support
me, and I am immensely grateful for you.

Finally, thank you to my launch team, who give valuable feedback
on typos and are happy to review upon release. It's lovely to hear from
them—you know who you are! You're amazing! I also love hearing
from all of my readers, so I welcome you to get in touch.

If you'd like to read more of my writing, please join my mailing
list at www.tjgreenauthor.com. You can get a free short story called
Jack's Encounter, describing how Jack met Fahey—a longer version of
the prologue in *Call of the King*—by subscribing to my newsletter.
You'll also get a free copy of *Excalibur Rises*, a short story prequel.
Additionally, you will receive free character sheets on all of my main
characters in White Haven Witches series—exclusive to my email list!

By staying on my mailing list, you'll receive free excerpts of my new
books and updates on new releases, as well as short stories and news of

giveaways. I'll also be sharing information about other books in this genre you might enjoy.

I encourage you to follow my Facebook page, T J Green. I post there reasonably frequently. In addition, I have a Facebook group called TJ's Inner Circle. It's a fab little group where I run giveaways and post teasers, so come and join us.

About the Author

I was born in England, in the Black Country, but moved to New Zealand in 2006. I lived near Wellington with my partner, Jase, and my cats, Sacha and Leia. However, in April 2022 we moved again! Yes, I like making my life complicated... I'm now living in the Algarve in Portugal, and loving the fabulous weather and people. When I'm not busy writing I read lots, indulge in gardening and shopping, and I love yoga.

Confession time! I'm a Star Trek geek—old and new—and love urban fantasy and detective shows. Secret passion—Columbo! Favourite Star Trek film is the *Wrath of Khan*, the original! Other top films—*Predator*, the original, and *Aliens*.

In a previous life I was a singer in a band, and used to do some acting with a theatre company. For more on me, check out a couple of my blog posts. I'm an old grunge queen, so you can read about my love of that on my blog: https://tjgreenauthor.com/about -a-girl-and-what-chris-cornell-means-to-me/. For more random news, read: https://tjgreenauthor.com/read-self-published-blog-tour-thin gs-you-probably-dont-know-about-me/

Why magic and mystery?

I've always loved the weird, the wonderful, and the inexplicable. Favourite stories are those of magic and mystery, set on the edges of the known, particularly tales of folklore, faerie, and legend—all the narratives that try to explain our reality.

The King Arthur stories are fascinating because they sit between reality and myth. They encompass real life concerns, but also cross boundaries with the world of faerie—or the Other, as I call it. There are green knights, witches, wizards, and dragons, and that's what I find particularly fascinating. They're stories that have intrigued people for generations, and like many others, I'm adding my own interpretation.

I love witches and magic, hence my second series set in beautiful Cornwall. There are witches, missing grimoires, supernatural threats, and ghosts, and as the series progresses, weirder stuff happens. The spinoff, White Haven Hunters, allows me to indulge my love of alchemy, as well as other myths and legends. Think Indiana Jones meets Supernatural!

Have a poke around in my blog posts and you'll find all sorts of posts about my series and my characters, and quite a few book reviews.

If you'd like to follow me on social media, you'll find me here:

f   facebook.com/tjgreenauthor/

𝓟   pinterest.com/Mount0live/

♪   tiktok.com/@tjgreenauthor

▶   youtube.com/@tjgreenauthor

g   goodreads.com/author/show/15099365.T_J_Green

◉   instagram.com/tjgreenauthor/

BB   bookbub.com/authors/tj-green

Other Books by T J Green

Rise of the King Series
A Young Adult series about a teen called Tom who is summoned to wake King Arthur. It's a fun adventure about King Arthur in the Otherworld!

Call of the King #1
The Silver Tower #2
The Cursed Sword #3

White Haven Hunters
The fun-filled spinoff to the White Haven Witches series! Featuring Fey, Nephilim, and the hunt for the occult.

Spirit of the Fallen #1
Shadow's Edge #2
Dark Star #3
Hunter's Dawn #4
Midnight Fire #5
Immortal Dusk #6

Storm Moon Shifters

This is an Urban Fantasy shifters spin-off in the White Haven World, and can be read as a standalone. There's a crossover of characters from my other series, and plenty of new ones. There is also a new group of witches who I love! It's set in London around Storm Moon, the club owned by Maverick Hale, alpha of the Storm Moon Pack. Audio will be available when I've organised myself!

Storm Moon Rising #1

Moonfell Witches

Witch fiction set in Moonfell, the gothic mansion in London. If you love magic, fantastic characters, urban fantasy and paranormal mysteries, you'll love this series. Join the Moonfell coven now!

The First Yule, a Moonfell Witches Novella.

Printed in Great Britain
by Amazon

35298855R00088